The Past Hunter

When Love Chases Her

2nd Edition

Ruthie Madison

Unique Pen Press
Edited by Martha Reineke of MK Editing Services
Image by

This book is a work of fiction. Names, characters, places and events are the product of the author's imagination or are used fictitiously.

The Past Hunter

Chapter 1

Julie ignored the intense longing in her heart as she drove along I-80 in southwestern Montana. As much as she loved Eric, what he had done was wrong. Why couldn't she call the police? It was her duty, but after he had carried a body in a rolled-up carpet, she panicked. She picked up her purse and car keys and walked out the door.

"Julie?" Eric had called.

She climbed in her car and drove as far away as possible, not even looking back. He had his chance at redeeming himself. He could have turned his phone off, but instead, he had answered the phone. Their date ended.

So why should she call him? Or answer the phone if he called her? Her phone lay next to her. She had only been on the road an hour and hadn't packed anything. She thought of calling her mom, and she picked up the phone just as it rang. It was Eric calling, and she let it go to voicemail. She changed her mind and decided to grab some clothing. She could easily let herself into the house with her key. Her parents would be asleep already. The dashboard clock read 10:30 pm.

At home, Julie unlocked the door and tiptoed inside. All the lights were off, so she used her pin light to help her find her room.

"Julie, is that you?" her mother called.

She pushed her door opened and took down her suitcase.

Her mother, Eleanor, gasped. "What are you doing?"

"I'm leaving Montana." No need to tell her why. She wouldn't understand. She threw her jeans in the suitcase.

"Why?" She sat on Julie's bed, frowning.

"I want a fresh start." Was she lying? She packed on impulse.

"What about your job? Have you told them?"

My job? Good question. It wasn't about her job. It was about Eric. Her mother wouldn't understand. She wiped a tear, as she would break her mother's heart.

Yet, her mom deserved to know the truth. She was getting a headache. "I...uh…" She sucked in and released a deep breath. "I'm leaving because of Eric." Her mother still frowned, and she hesitated to say what came next. "I think...he killed a man."

Eleanor shook her head. "I can't believe that."

She was right. Her mother didn't witness it. She did. "How much do you even know about him?" she barked. She picked up her suitcase and ran off to her car before her mother could stop her. She was twenty-four. It was time to move out anyway.

As she drove, she covered her mouth, fighting back tears. As hard as it was, she had to leave, or she would end up staying. Eric might ask her parents where Julie was or why she left town. She couldn't risk him finding out that she called the deputy after all, he could have killed that man. *I hope they arrest him. Serves him right.*

Julie's heart pounded. She had a whole new life ahead of her. What would she find where she was going? New friends? She touched her heart. She would miss Charity and Faith. She graduated from high school with them, but Charity had moved back to Helena, and Faith had married a rancher's son named Slick Rick. How lucky she was. Julie wanted to marry Eric, but it never got that far. Would she meet someone new?

The stars glittered in the night sky with their radiant light as Julie drove through town. A bright neon sign on A to Z Pharmacy caught Julie's eyes. Her pulse raced. She could dye her hair red, and Eric wouldn't be able to recognize her. What a brilliant plan! She couldn't wait to find the right color of hair dye. She parked her car in front of the store.

"Welcome to A to Z Pharmacy. Can I help you?" The clerk's unexpected voice made her jump. "Sorry. I didn't mean to startle you. Can I help you find something?" The bright young clerk with light blue hair stared at her.

"Red hair dye, please." She smiled.

"Right over here." She showed Julie a row of red hair dye. "Are you in some kind of trouble?" She grinned. Her eyes wild with delight.

Did she look like a criminal to her? The clerk could have had a criminal past. Who would dye their hair blue? Julie suppressed a giggle, and she kept her opinion to herself. "No. Just wanting to start my life anew." She offered her a smile.

The clerk grinned, nodding. "I hear you on that."

###

She's gone! When he returned to his date with Julie, her purse was gone, and she was not in his room or on the couch. *Where could she have gone?* He ran outside calling her name. "JULIE! JULIE!" *Did she leave?* Eric turned on a flashlight. "JULIE!!!!"

The neighbor's dog barked, and a light turned on in their house. A woman looked out the window. "I saw a woman leave your house an hour ago!"

An hour ago? Oh no! What if Drew found her first? He couldn't handle that. Drew hated Eric, and he would do anything to destroy him, including taking Julie from him.

Eric hopped into his truck and called Julie on his cell phone. He should not have taken that call. He had planned on asking her to move in with him since Drew swore he would take Julie away from him. Beads of sweat streaked down his face.

"Hi. This is Julie. Leave a message."

Eric raked his free hand through his hair. *Pick up, woman!* "Julie, where are you? Please call me!" He hit end call.

When he arrived at her parents place, he hopped out and stormed to the door. He didn't care who he woke. He banged on the door. Julie's jeep was not in the driveway.

"Eric?" Her mother opened the door and frowned. "What's wrong?"

"I need to find Julie! Is she here? Please say yes."

"I haven't seen her. I thought she was with you." Her eyes showed concerned.

He shook his head. "I wouldn't be here if she was!" he snapped. "Sorry. I'm beside myself with worry. Please let me know if she calls."

Eleanor's brow wrinkled. She was just as concern as he was. He tried to calm down, but his mind was going a million miles an hour trying to figure out where she went. "You might try Faith. Maybe she is staying the night over there."

He nodded. "It's worth a try. Sorry to bother you," he muttered.

On his way to his house, he called Faith instead. Rick answered. "Hi, Eric. What's up?"

"Is Julie there?"

"No. She's not. Weren't you on a date?"

"Yes, but I had to attend to business. Sorry to bother you." He hit end call.

After driving around and calling Julie's friends on his phone, his throat closed up. Had Julie mentioned anything about travelling? Had he missed something? He raked his hand through his hair. *Okay, Young. Calm down. It doesn't do you any good to worry.* No, it didn't. What happened before he took the call? He disappointed her by taking that call. Did she leave him for that? His father's word haunted him:

"You're worthless, boy! You hear me? No woman would want you when you are a man. You are a coward, plain and simple." His father lifted a whip as if to strike him. "Now go out there and prove your worth!"

Was his father right? His throat ached.

Eric stopped at a local tavern. A drink sounded good about now. He stepped out and headed toward the entrance.

A country band played on a platform, and patrons filled the tables and the bar, leaving a couple of empty spaces. Eric sat down, and a waiter attended to him. "What can I get you?" Eric told him he wanted a classic Miller, and the bartender filled his order.

The golden elixir was like the soul-soothing nectar of God. He was alone. No one with him. No Julie. He sighed. Julie deserved better. He failed her. He failed her as a protector. Now Drew would find out she was an easy target. A smile built up on his face. He won't find her. If *he* couldn't neither would Drew. It didn't comfort him. His throat ached constantly.

"I'm out of my mind." He drank a few swallows.

"Yes, you are." Drew's voice chilled the air. "Where's that pretty lady of yours? Did she leave you?" He sneered.

Eric scooted over as if he didn't want Drew next to him. "Leave me alone, Drew," he mumbled.

"I can hardly hear you, Young. You need to speak louder. Bartender, give him another beer."

Eric rose to his feet, but Drew pushed him down.

"Leave me alone."

"I'm not through with you. You are going to have another beer to end your misery."

"What do you care? You hate me."

"I don't hate you. I despise you!" He swore It's your own fault for that mess you are in." He pushed the beer to him. "Now you will tell me where Julie is, or I'll smash your brain in." Drew balled his fist, but Eric didn't flinch.

He tried to laugh but couldn't. He got up and ran out the door. He didn't want a fight. He desired no company.

"YOU ARE A COWARD, YOUNG! YOU HEAR ME!"

Chapter 2

A cell phone chimed, waking Eric up. He wondered where he was. It was still dark out, and he was in his car. He picked up his phone. "Hello?"

"Eric, Julie was just here. She said something that didn't make sense." Eleanor sounded frantic.

"What did she tell you?" He rubbed his head, pounding because of a headache.

"She thinks you killed a man."

Her words restricted his breathing. *She thought I killed a man?* How did she come to that conclusion? Had she seen him? He was a good man. Full of love and care for his woman. Had someone poisoned her mind against him? Drew?

He could feel the color drain from his face. He needed to find her. "Eleanor, she knows me better than that!"

"I know, but that's what she said, and she packed her bag and left. What happened with you two?"

Julie packed? His head spun, and his insides quivered. Drew would find her. *Oh God! I need to find her!* He was getting hot. Too hot. "She just left? Did she say where?"

"She wouldn't tell us any more. Eric, what's going on?"

"She's not safe."

"Jesus can keep her safe."

His stomach had a slight quiver. Would He? Eric might not get to her in time. "Mrs. Henshaw, do you know any place Julie would love to visit?"

"When she was a little girl, she wanted to go to Disneyland."

Eric shook his head. She wouldn't take off just to go to Disneyland. *God, I hope she calls me.* "Thank you, Mrs. Henshaw." He ended the call and dialed one more time, hoping she would answer.

###

Rascal Flatts' "God Bless the Broken Road" sounded on her phone. It was Eric again. Should she answer? She cleared her throat. "Hello?"

"Julie, where are you?"

"Eric, stop worrying about me. Worry about you. It's over between us."

"I'm sorry I took the phone call."

She boiled over upon hearing his apology. She should have called 911. Was that why he thought she left? It was a lot more than that. She hung up and called the deputy. If he wouldn't do it, she would. She should have a long time ago.

"Gallatin County Police Department. May I help you?"

"This is Julie Henshaw. I'd like to report a crime."

"Okay. What crime did you witness?"

"It was at the Old Fox Ranch. I saw Eric Young bringing a body in a rolled-up carpet into the house."

"Are you sure there is a body in there?"

"I overheard him talk about it. He was acting suspicious. Check the cellar. That's where they took it. Please don't tell him who called. I wish to remain anonymous. And I'm leaving Montana."

"At what time did this happen?"

"Nine at night. He left around seven thirty. We were on a date, and he took a call from Craig."

"What's Craig's last name?"

"Muldare."

"Okay. We will check it out."

"Alright." She hit end call.

Once they put Eric behind bars, she could go back to Bozeman and work another two weeks before she moved. She needed to do this. She cleared her throat. She wished she hadn't made that call. She had acted out of anger. What about justice for the family? The dead man may have done something to deserve death, but only God should decide. No man should kill a human being. She only did what was right.

"I should have called the police while I was there."

Regret swept in like a flood. She tried to push her actions out of her mind. How could she have done that? In spite of what he done, she still loved him. How could she turn on him like that? She laid her hand on her breastbone.

Julie yawned. She needed sleep before returning home. She would do the right thing and give her employer a two weeks' notice.

###

"Open up! This is the deputy!"

Adrenaline shot through his system. This was it! The police were going to arrest him. He took some quick, shallow breaths. He needed to calm down, but how? He couldn't face the deputy. He came out of his room just as they pushed the door in.

"We have a warrant to search your property!"

"What's...what's going on?" He followed them, trying to stay inconspicuous.

"We received a call from an anonymous tipper that you have a dead body in your cellar. Please lead us to the body."

Who had called them? Had Craig turned him in? He felt the color drain from his face. Anonymous tipper? His life was over. "No need." He led them out to the cellar and waited for them to arrest him. *Only one person could have known. How could she?*

The deputy unrolled the carpet and discovered the body of Clarence O'Connor dead on the floor. Their faces drained of color, and they looked at one another in shock. "Put your hands behind your back. You are under arrest." They cuffed him and read him his rights, then they led him out.

###

The rooster crowed. Julie had betrayed Eric. She couldn't imagine Eric behind bars. Eric wouldn't even hurt a fly, let alone kill a man. Couldn't she have stayed to find out what happened? *What have I done?*

Her mother was in the kitchen making breakfast. Julie had no appetite. The aroma of bacon and eggs drifted from the kitchen to her room and nauseated her. Her father walked past her room as if he didn't notice her there. Julie overheard them talking in the next room.

"Good morning, honey!" Her mother greeted her father.

"Julie up yet?" he asked.

"Last I saw, she was asleep."

"Did she work it out with him?"

"When she came home last night, she said nothing. Just went to her room and closed the door."

Julie stretched and yawned. It was Saturday, and she had the day off. Still, she would give her two weeks' notice. After that, she would disappear and make new friends elsewhere. Her house was her prison. She could never forgive herself. Tears leaked out of her eyes as she lay her head on the pillow.

"Julie, breakfast is ready!"

"Not hungry."

Footsteps came near. Her father stood in her doorway. "Are you feeling okay?"

"No. I wish I never came back...not after what I have done."

"What are you talking about?"

"I...called. I..." She sniffed. "Eric's in jail..." she cried. "I'm a horrible girlfriend...I thought he did it."

"Sweetie, you're not making sense. Are you saying that you put him in jail?" He sat on her bed.

She nodded. "I saw...body. Assumed...worst."

His face showed no emotion. He stared at the ground. "Well, maybe they will clear him." He sat up. "You need to put it past you. You can't live in regret all your life." He walked out of her room.

Julie's stomach grumbled. She decided she would try to eat. She got up and headed out to the kitchen. "I'm going to take a trip when I feel up to it. Start my life over." She sat in front of a plate of bacon and eggs.

Her breakfast tasted like sandpaper. She swallowed it with juice and forced herself to eat.

Her mother looked on with compassion. "Honey, the best thing you could do is give it to God. We all make mistakes, but it doesn't surprise God. If you have sinned, confess it. If you feel guilty, give him your guilt. He is there to listen to you and to forgive you."

Julie nodded. What her mother said made sense, but she couldn't find strength to forgive herself. She didn't witness Eric killing the man. He might have aided Craig. If that was the case, then the deputy needed to investigate him. She would pray and ask God to help her let go of her regrets.

After she ate what she could, she went to her room and knelt. "Jesus, I am sorry for what I have done. I was angry. If Eric hadn't called me, I would not have turned him in. I pray he would find it in his heart to forgive me."

She drew upon God's strength as she dressed. Her body warmed up, and her heartbeat increased. Today, she would go to the diner and hand in her letter of resignation. She had wanted to visit him behind bars, but she had made up on her mind to wait on that. He might not have killed that man, but he still helped.

###

The weight of regret lifted as waitresses took orders from customers. Jordan smiled as she noticed Julie. "Hi! I didn't know you work today."

"Actually, I am here to give my two weeks' notice."

Jordan gasped. "Why?"

She put on a happy face. "I want to start my life anew."

Jordan's smile faded. "What about Eric?"

She stared at the floor. "He's in jail."

She gasped. "For what?"

"Murdering a man." She grimaced. "Is Jay back there?" Jordan didn't respond, but nodded to her question. Julie made her way to the kitchen. Jay, a man in his late thirties stood over a frying pan. "Hi, Jay."

. "Morning, Julie. What can I do for you?" He flipped the eggs over.

"I'm resigning. I'm giving my two weeks' notice."

Jay frowned.

"Is that right, Julie?" His wife Julz approached her. "Is everything okay?"

Her smile froze. "Yes! I'm fine! I just need to start my life again. I'll be here for two more weeks, so you'll see Monday." She stormed out.

Did I make the right choice? She asked herself that as she climbed into her car. If she didn't, how could she get a job elsewhere? Although, she had not planned on waitressing all her life, she didn't want to jeopardize her chance at getting a new job.

As she drove, the small white church with a steeple on top lightened Julie's heart. It gave her a sense of calm. She parked in front of the church and headed toward the sanctuary. Though tomorrow she would attend service, she needed a place to pray and sensed His presence.

Light shone through the stained glass windows of the sanctuary as if God's glory had lit up the room. Every pew emptied of people, Julie approached the altar and knelt at the cross. Tears trickled down her face. "Daddy, I need you. My heart aches. Help me to move on. Help me make right decisions. I don't deserve Eric. I don't blame him if he is angry at me. I'm willing to let him go."

"That is a beautiful prayer." Pastor Blake knelt beside her.

Her chest fluttered. He would listen to her without judgment. Her parents wouldn't understand, but she had known him since he replaced Pastor Holland six years ago. "Can we talk? I need someone to talk to."

"You want sit in the pew or in my office?"

"Pew is fine."

He stood up then offered his hand to help her up. She grabbed his warm hand. Pastor Blake led her to a pew, his blue eyes searching hers for what was on her heart.

She took a deep breath. "Friday, Eric and I were in his home watching a movie. I had anticipated a proposal from him. We've dated for over two years. I knew about his troubled life, but I thought he put it behind him. His cell phone rang and my heart shrank. He took a call from a friend of his and ended our date as he left. I stayed because I didn't think he would be gone long. I fell asleep and woke up to some commotion."

"Okay. So Eric ended your date, and you were upset."

"Yes. Very, but I was ready to forgive him when he came back."

He nodded. "What happened?"

"Eric is a good man, Pastor Blake, but I couldn't understand why he brought a rolled-up carpet to the back of the house. I heard him say something about a body, and I freaked out."

He raised his eyebrows. "A body?"

She nodded. "Yes. I didn't confront him. I chickened out. I left the house and drove for an hour...."

Pastor Blake said nothing. His mind seemed far away as if he was deep in thought. Was he searching for the words to say? His eyes showed concern, and he started to speak but closed his mouth. "Have you talked to your parents?"

"As I said, they wouldn't understand. They love Eric!"

"May I pray for you?"

She nodded, then closed her eyes.

"Heavenly Father, fill Julie with your love and peace. Give her the assurance to know you forgive her. Help her to forgive herself and to move on. She needs you, Father. And help her to forgive Eric. If he is the one, for her, let there be reconciliation between them. If not, help them to move on. I also pray for Eric. That he may know you in his time of need. May he need to hear the gospel he so desperately needs to hear in Jesus name? Amen."

All the weight she had carried, lifted off her shoulders. How ironic that Eric lost his freedom while she gained freedom from her regrets. Tears fell and she embraced her handsome pastor. With a smile, she said, "How is Belinda?"

"She is doing super!" He grinned. "Feeling better?"

"Yes. Thank you for listening to me."

"You're more than welcome. See you in church tomorrow."

"Same to you!" She walked out with a spring in her step, but she would still leave Montana.

Chapter 3

Dressed in prison garb, the guard led Eric down the walkway. Prisoners behind shiny bars uttered profanity. He was a low-life, just as they were. He deserved what was coming to him. His old man was right. He was worth nothing.

The guard unlocked the door. "Louis, you have a cell mate!" He removed the handcuffs from Eric and locked him behind bars.

Eric's chest ached. If Julie ratted on him, he deserved it. He doubted he would see her again.

"So what are you in for?" Louis interrupted his introspection.

"Murder," he mumbled.

"What did you say? Speak louder!" Louis flexed his muscular arms and crossed them. "They have me doing time for drug dealing and child molestation." He laughed. "I'm here a long time."

His eyes widened. Why would he talk to a low-life like him? "Murder."

"Wow! You should be proud of yourself!" He mocked him.

What did he have to be proud about? He was a lousy boyfriend, a lousy rancher—why did he ranch in the first place? The ranch belonged to his father. Doing time sounded better than taking care of cattle.

"Here are the rules. I get the top bunk. You get the bottom. You understand. I don't want you touching my bed."

Eric nodded. He climbed into his bed and curled up, wishing to go unnoticed.

Later in the day, the prisoners banged on the bars. Eric wished they would quiet down, but the banging grew louder.

"Young, you have a visitor. You have an hour." A guard jingled his keys at Eric's cell.

A visitor? Who would want to visit a low-life like him? His father died long ago, and he hadn't seen Julie since yesterday. His chest ached. He missed her.

The guard handcuffed him and led him down the hall to the visiting area.

Randy sat at a round table watching him. His face full of sorrow and compassion. Why? Why would anyone have compassion on him? He even failed his ranch hands.

The guard seated him then left.

"Eric, I couldn't believe when I heard the news. Tell me it ain't so. What about Julie?"

"Julie can live without me," he mumbled.

"You need to stop feeling sorry for yourself! Your old man is not here. You have people that love you!"

"Love me? Julie left me!"

"Your friends love you like a brother. You, John, and I grew up together! Our fathers were ranchers!"

"My life is not worth anything."

"You need to snap out of it!"

Eric flinched. Was his hour up? He wanted to leave.

"Listen, we are going to get you a good attorney. There is no way you have killed that man." Randy reached for his hand. "Can I pray for you?"

Eric nodded, but he wouldn't close his eyes. As far as he was concerned, God wouldn't show interest in him.

"Dear, Lord. Eric needs you. We don't know what really happened, but you do. Show him your love and your light. Help him through his dark times. I pray in Jesus's name. Amen."

Randy's prayer lifted some weight off his shoulders. He needed a friend who cared, even if he didn't think he was worth friendship. Maybe Louis would befriend him. "Thank you," he mumbled.

###

Sunday morning, Eric looked down as the prison guard led him and the prisoners to the chapel. They had him chained, thinking he would get away. Where was he going? He belonged here. He sat next to Louis, but not close. *Better keep your eyes on the ground. Don't get your hopes up.*

He had little hope. No sermon would set him free from his own prison. He had sealed his own fate Friday night. His father had often told him in not so many words that God didn't like low-life people like himself, so he kept a blank face.

"We are all unworthy," the gray-haired chaplain began, but with a sparkle in his eyes, "of God's love. We all have done things we regret..."

His body heated up. What was the preacher? A mind reader? How would he know what he had done? Who told him? Eric sat rigid as he sucked in his cheeks. "Yeah right," he mumbled.

"Amen!" Louis bellowed.

"But God's word is true. We all have sinned. Even I have sinned. Even I have done undeserving things just as any of you. I want to read from the book of John. This is where Jesus was about to be crucified. Peter was going to deny Jesus three times..."

Eric relaxed. The message woke him as the preacher spoke of a man who denied Jesus three times. Peter had done it too! Had Peter felt worthless? Did he think he was not worthy to follow Jesus? All his life he thought God wouldn't show interest in him.

###

Two weeks later, Julie shivered as she drove. She had the heat on, but the chill wouldn't go away. Cars zoomed past her, but no one looked like they were tail gating her. So why did she feel as if someone was following her? She couldn't wait for morning to come.

The night dragged on. It seemed like daylight would never come. The time on her dashboard read 10p.m. Was she in southern California yet? A sign ahead read: "Welcome to Marysville, population 12,200." Marysville was far from southern California! She let out an impatient sigh.

A loud sound came from her car. *Bang!*

Her adrenaline shot through her system as she pulled over onto the shoulder. Julie opened her hood and walked around to check for any damages. She had no clue where to begin. *God, please send help!* Who was she kidding? Even the cars that passed by were not more two or three at time, and they just zoomed by. Should she call for help?

Not more than fifteen minutes later, a white car slowed. A medium-height man with wavy, brown hair, wearing a white dress shirt and a pair of khakis stepped out and walked to her car. "You need help?"

All her bodily tension went away. God had answered her prayer by sending a man who reminded her of Eric. The one man she had felt safe with. "Yes. I think my car died."

"Let me have a look." He walked to her engine and checked it. Soon, he straightened up. "Your timing belt is broken."

Her mouth scrunched up. "My what?"

"Timing belt. You need to get a new one. Call your insurance and have them send a tow truck." He smiled.

"You don't know how glad I am you stopped. I waited out here for a half hour and no one cared."

"God told me to stop. I was on my way home. Were you heading some place?"

This angel had lightened her heart. Not only did he attract her, but he heard from God! Out here at night—in the middle of night. Just a bit earlier, she had felt a chill, but his presence brought warmth to her. "Southern California."

"You have a long ways to go. You're in Marysville, California. It's late." He took out his wallet and gave her one hundred-dollar bill. "This should be enough for one night in a motel."

That was more than she made for a tip in one day! She smiled her thanks then she called her insurance company.

"Triple A Road Service. May I help you?"

"My timing belt stopped working. It went bang. I'm outside Marysville on State Highway 20 past E. 17th Street can you send a tow?"

"And who is calling?"

"Julie Henshaw." She gazed upward as the operator typed on her keyboard. *Thank you, God!*

"A tow truck should be there in ten minutes. Hang in there."

She smiled to Eric's "twin." God had a sense of humor sending him her way. "Okay. Thank you." She ended the call. "And thank you."

He gave a gratifying sigh. "You're welcome." He walked to his car. "Want to wait inside?"

"I'm fine."

"Okay." He climbed in.

###

Julie's gaze was on the oncoming traffic, but wouldn't she be looking in the direction of Marysville? Why was she looking toward Truckee? Or even...Nevada? Did she come from Nevada?

"Offer to stand with her."

He checked his watch. He would prefer if she was out of the elements and safe from crime. He stepped out and walked over to her. "I'll wait with you."

Her mouth dropped open as she looked him over. "You don't have to."

"I want to."

She smiled. "Okay. I'm Julie." She had the prettiest of blue eyes; his heart fluttered. He wished it hadn't.

"Andrew."

"So how long have you known Jesus?"

He took some easy breaths, thinking about that day. God changed his life and helped him become a better person sixteen years ago. Perhaps he could help Julie. "Sixteen years."

"What was the factor?"

"We could talk about it in my car if you like."

"Never mind." She glanced away.

Second time she turned him down. *Does she think I'll assault or abduct her?* His pulse picked up. What was her reason for coming out here? "So what brings you to California?"

Chapter 4

Ever since the preacher spoke, Eric wanted to know more about Peter. What was Peter's life like growing up? Did he have an abusive father? Did he ever feel worthless? *He denied Jesus three times.* Whom had Eric denied—had he kept to himself to not acknowledge?

"You deny who you are."

Eric raised his voice at the unexpected voice. It made him sick and gave him a headache. "I know who I am. I'm a low-life. You don't have to tell me."

"What's that?" Louis asked from his bed below.

"Nothing," he mumbled.

Louis chuckled. "Okay."

He wanted nothing to do with ranching anymore since Julie left him. He denied anything to do with his friends, who by the way, stood by him—regardless. Including Randy. He squeezed his eyes shut. *Let me see him again! Please, God!* Eric laughed. Why would God answer him?

"What's funny, cowboy?"

"Why would God care about me?"

"Why would He care about any of us? The Bible states we have all sinned and fallen short the glory of God."

"All?" He raised his eyebrows. "Even Julie?

"No one is perfect, but God is."

Julie was perfect in every way. The way her long blonde hair flowed down her sides and back. The way her lips puckered when she wanted a kiss. And her blue eyes, all perfect in his eyes. How could she not be perfect?

"She betrayed you," an accusing voice told him.

Eric frowned. "I guess you're right. So what's the remedy?"

"Accepting Jesus in your heart."

"Then I'm sinless?"

"No, but God forgives when we ask for it. He gives us the grace and mercy that we need."

Grace and mercy. He never heard of that. He wanted to know more. And he would. "Thanks, man."

Eric continued to devour the Bible.

Later in the day, the prison guard led the prisoners to the visiting area as he announced that a choir was going to sing some songs.

Eric swallowed a few times as he sat by Louis and Rico. Rico acknowledged his presence, as he smiled. Did he like gospel music? Eric nodded.

"Good evening. We're from The Chapel of Grace," the choir director announced. "We would like to sing a few songs. Our first song is a classic, 'The Wonderful Grace of Jesus.' Hit it!"

As music played, the choir sang. "Wonderful of grace of Jesus, greater than all my sin..."

Eric sat motionless. He swallowed as his mouth hung open. Gone were his worries and cares as he absorbed himself in the lyrics.

"Oh, the wonderful grace of Jesus reaches me..."

Goosebumps slid across his body, causing him to shiver. If only Randy and John were here to experience it with him. He sensed an awesome presence he could not describe. The prisoners around him blurred into the background, but the singers had their eyes on him.

"Deeper than the mighty rolling sea...."

Eric closed his eyes and took a deep breath. *Jesus, I need you. I need your grace. If you come and live with me, I'll do my best to serve you.*

A peace he had never sensed before filled his heart, and joy flooded his soul. All his shame and feelings of worthlessness washed away, and Jesus filled him with a sense of purpose in his life. "Jesus, I want to do right by you."

A hand slapped him on the back. "Way to go, man!" Louis said.

"It won't last. He'll come back to himself when he finds he's still stuck here," Rico scorned him.

"Rico, I really don't care what you think. You scorned me ever since you saw me, but not anymore." Eric glared at him.

After the choir sang, Eric wanted to talk to the choir director, but the prison guard led them back to their cells.

The next morning, as the prisoners waited for their breakfast, Eric absorbed what he could find the Bible. The song about grace intrigued him. As he skimmed through the New Testament, he held his breath. "First and Second Peters?" He wasted no time turning to First Peter. As soon as he read grace and mercy, all his worries ceased as he devoured the two letters.

"Breakfast! Come and get your grub! Young, you have a visitor. Stand with your hands behind your back." A guard walked down the hall, as he let each prisoner out to eat.

Hope filled his chest. He complied as the prison guard handcuffed him and led him down to the visiting area. Last week, John had come and prayed with him. He coveted his prayers.

Prisoners liked their visitors, and he was no exception. He had a good feeling about his visitor. Would it be Julie this time? He wanted to reconnect with her, and he hoped she would forgive him.

As the guard led him to the table, a man sat in a business suit. *A lawyer?* Randy had said he could get an attorney, but how could an attorney help him? *Did Craig confess?* He sat with his eyes on him.

"Hello, Eric. I'm a defense attorney. My name is Lionel Roseberg, and I am here to help you get your release."

"But I confessed to the crime."

The attorney's smile made his heart feel light. "I'm sure you did, but your friend who hired me believes you are innocent. So we are going to prove that. I just need information from you. You haven't had a trial yet. Right?"

"No, sir. I'm waiting,"

"We are also going to get you out on bail. Your friend is paying for it."

"Which one?"

"Randall Johnson."

Warmth's filled Eric's heart. He had a friend on his side, and Randy made good on his promise. He wanted an early release, but he wouldn't betray Craig. He was all for helping out. "I can tell you what I know."

"We will need an audio and video tape."

Eric nodded as another man came in with the equipment and set it up.

"Did you or did you not kill Clarence O'Connor?"

He tensed up. Could he do it? Could he say no and clear himself? He had gotten used to prison life, but his heart was for Julie. He still felt the need to protect her. Early release? Bail? Did he want a bail bond? *Is Craig more important than me?*

"You're stalling."

"I... uh." He squeezed his eyes shut. *Help me, God.* "I didn't, but I helped."

"You helped?"

"He came to me for help."

"Who did you help?"

"Craig Muldare. I was on a date with my girlfriend when he called. He said, 'I shot a man! Now I'm doomed.' He panicked."

"Why did he shoot him?"

"He owed money to Clarence, but when he didn't have the money, Clarence threatened to take his wife away from him. He threatened to smear him. Craig got scared, and in self-defense, he shot the man."

"Doesn't sound like self-defense to me."

"Craig was defending himself and his wife from him. He didn't mean to. He got scared. When he realized what he had done, he thought he killed in self-defense. He called me while I was on a date and asked me to help.

"And why would you help him?"

"Because he's helped me," he said with strong conviction.

"So what did you do?"

His belly knotted up. He failed Julie. He let her down. He broke her heart. She had begged him to not leave. *Julie's gone.* It was all his fault. He deserved what he got. *Grace. Grace that is deeper than the roiling sea.* A warmth replaced the dullness of his chest. God had forgiven him. As he continued, he sensed God gave him grace to come clean. "I let down the only woman I have ever loved. I drove to the man's office. We both rolled up the dead man in the carpet and took him to my house. My friend and I didn't want to draw attention to ourselves, so we walked quietly to the back...and I guess that's when she saw us."

"Craig Muldare."

Everything he had kept inside concerning Craig all spilled out, leaving him empty and light. "Yes." Eric bowed his head.

Silence filled the room.

###

After the tow truck driver dropped Julie off at Ace's Auto Repair, Andrew waited for her in his car. Every time she looked at him, butterflies would dance in her stomach. Why? She had gotten out of a relationship. She wasn't looking for romance. She needed to guard her heart. She also didn't need another "Eric" in her life. Was that her problem? Her flesh got in the way?

Julie ambled to his car and climbed in. The motel wouldn't be far, so she could just sit quietly as he drove. She secured the seatbelt over herself.

"Motel 8?"

She smiled as she nodded.

As he drove, he turned the radio on. "Up next we have TobyMac with *Move. Keep Walking,*" the DJ announced.

Julie perked up. The music pouring from the radio was one she never heard. The beat and rhythm were nothing like gospel or country. She raised her eyebrows. "You listen to this kind of music?"

"Most times." He smiled. "Why?"

"I never heard it before."

"What do you like to listen to?"

"Country. Gospel."

"Kirk Franklin?"

She shook her head. "Erne Hasse, Bill Gaither."

"The Gaither Vocal Band is cool. My parents listen to them."

"I was raised on country, but when I became a Christian, I started listening to my mom's CDs. She collects them."

"I see. Do you like Randy Travis?"

She gave him a nod, leaning in. "Brad Paisley, George Straight, and Rascal Flatts."

"God Bless the Broken Road that led me straight to you."

A tear fell down her face. "That song played when I was working as a waitress the night Eric walked in." She touched her heart.

"Obviously, you still love him."

"No, I'm over him. Just trying to get over it."

###

His throat tightened. Was there something he could do to help her? He had been there. His last girlfriend stabbed him in his heart when she went after another man. "Did...did...you tell him?"

"On the phone." She stared out the window. He could see she still longed for him; was she really over him? Something told him it would be awhile before she could date again. While they had waited for the tow truck, she had told him that Eric had committed a crime, but he sensed regret in her voice. She had come out to California to start her life again. He could be a friend to her, but nothing more. She would need friends. Beth, his brother's girlfriend, would make a great friend. *Father God, thank you for Julie. I ask that you help Julie connect with Beth so that Beth can help her to grow in her faith. Amen.*

When he arrived at the motel, he got out, and like a gentleman, he opened the door for her. "I want to keep in touch. Can I have your cell phone number?"

Her eyes widened in surprise, and the corner of her mouth lifted. She opened her purse, took out a pen and sheet of paper, and wrote it down. "Don't lose it."

"Just to keep in touch, nothing more."

"I understand." She stepped out as he went to get her luggage and garment bag out of the back.

What kind of dresses does Julie wear? She had said she was from Montana, but for some reason he conjured an image of a cowgirl. *Is it because of the straw hat on her hair of red?* He shook his head. *Why am I thinking this?* He just wanted friendship.

"Thanks for the help."

"You're welcome." He walked to his car and climbed in.

Chapter 5

That night, Julie had planned to stay one night, but after the friendliness and kindness he had shown her, she changed her mind. "How much for a week for one bed?"

"Five hundred dollars."

She gasped, wondering if she had that much on hand; even with the one hundred dollar bill Andrew gave her, it was more than she could afford. A week at Best Western in Bozeman was less than that. She would have to write a check. "Do you accept checks?"

He shook his head and frowned. "Cash or credit cards."

She reached into her purse and took her wallet out. She would need a job soon. She had some money in the bank, but if she didn't find a job, she would have to live in her car or go home. She handed the clerk her Visa card.

He swiped it and waited a minute. "Go ahead and date and sign your name."

She did so, and he gave her a key.

"Room 11."

"Thank you."

###

The next morning, hope filled her heart. She lifted her hands in praise. "Jesus, thank you for today. I ask that you would guide my steps and that you would grant me favor where ever I go. If this is where you want me, then open doors for me in your name. Amen."

Before Julie applied for a job anywhere, she needed to check on her car. Ace wasn't open last night, but they would be that morning. She stepped out of her room and started walking north to the repair shop.

A white car slowed and Andrew poked his head out the window. "Heading to the repair shop?"

Julie perked up. "Yes, I am!"

"I can give you a ride. I have some time before I head for work."

The repair shop was only a few blocks away. Andrew knew that. He didn't have to go out of his way to offer her a ride. Taking this as a positive sign that he wanted to help his friend, it lightened her heart. A calm feeling came over her as she neared his car. "Good morning." She opened the door.

"I'm sorry. I should have opened it for you."

"Don't worry." She strapped herself in. "I'm going to look for a job."

"Books and Gifts is hiring. I could take you over there, but they open at nine."

Julie raised her eyebrows. "Books and Gifts? Are they far from the motel?"

He nodded. "A mile."

"Maybe I could use the exercise. I haven't eaten yet, so you can drop me off, and I'll walk there. What's the address?"

"451 West Main Street."

She took out her cell phone and jotted it down in her notes. "Thanks."

###

Andrew arrived in front of Ace Auto Repair. Two men were inside getting ready to work on another car, but not hers. *Should I go in with her? It might help.* "Some mechanics would love to rip you off. Let me go with you." He stepped out and walked to the mechanics. "Good morning, my friend here needs a new timing belt on her car. Can you replace hers?"

The bald-headed mechanic looked her over and gave her a quirky smile. Andrew's pulse quickened. Did the mechanic think he could scam her in his presence? He wouldn't allow it. "Please treat her with the same dignity, you'd treat male clients." He crossed his arms, frowning.

The mechanic picked up on his irritation and backed off. "No problem. We'll do so." He walked over to the jeep that waited in front of the shop. He opened the trunk and checked the inside. "It will take a couple of days to get a new part. Do you have a phone number where I can reach you?"

Andrew handed him a business card before Julie could say a word. She gasped. "I'll notify her." He offered a smile.

The mechanic took the card, smiling as he walked away.

As Andrew led her to his car, he said, "I'm just looking out for my new friend. I saw the way he looked at you." His eyebrows drew together.

Julie's eyes filled with a soft and warm glow. "I'm...speechless. Thank you." A smile built on her face, adding to that shade of red he loved on her.

Across from the repair shop was a McDonald's. *Do they have one in Montana?* "Are you hungry?"

"I was thinking of going there anyway. I can just walk there." His body language indicated his discomfort. I'm sure you have eaten already...unless you want to treat." She covered her mouth. "Sorry."

He shrugged then he led her across the street.

The menu had some interesting breakfast items. He rarely ate at fast food, and he hadn't planned on eating here. He wondered if she liked fast food. Her eyes fixed on the menu. "See anything you like?"

"Pancake breakfast." She gave him a five then walked to a table.

His jaws and facial muscles tightened. Julie didn't have to do that. He could've afforded breakfast for two. Then again, she could've done it because she didn't wanted him to think—or construe it as a date. Was that it? His muscles loosened. He needed to relax.

"Can I help the next person?"

###

Her pulse was on a race course to win. Andrew must have thought she couldn't fend for herself. The way he insisted that he talk to the mechanic. She'd had her car repaired before. Did he think she was clueless? Why couldn't she just write him off as cocky and arrogant? She didn't need that in her life. She wasn't needy either. She wanted to give him a piece of her mind.

"Order number—"

"Do you think I'm dumb?" She folded her arms.

"What?" Confusion flashed in his eyes.

"Seems to me that you think you are God's gift to women."

"No. I think God wanted me to help you."

"Oh really?" She raised her eyebrows.

"Why are you acting this way?" He acted hurt, but she didn't buy it. "Okay. I wish you best." He walked to another table.

A lump formed in her throat. Why did she have to be so angry? Was she thinking he was like Eric? Was that where it came from? Andrew may look like him, but he was no way quiet like Eric was. He had done more for her than Eric had done in his life time. She needed to make up to him. "I'm sorry I acted that way. You must think I'm...ungrateful." She joined him at his table. "What's going on in your life?"

Andrew looked deep in thought. "I'm sorry too. I should've asked, instead of assuming." A smile tugged at the corner of his lips. "And I'm mad at myself too."

"You are?"

He nodded. "My parents raised my brother and me to respect women. I even have a sister. When I did that for someone, she walked all over me."

His advantage squeezed her ribs like ketchup in a bottle. She wanted to have a sibling. How many times had she ever wished for a little sister, to maybe share some of the blame instead of being the child that was always wrong? Or how about the times she would have missed out sharing secrets? Life seemed so unfair. "Lucky you." She mumbled, her face turning red.

"Why am I lucky? Because a woman walked all over me?"

Was it hot in here or what? Julie fanned herself. *Huh—what?* He had exposed her ignorance? What was he talking about? Siblings. Women—*Oh*. "No! Not that! You have siblings; I don't. Is she younger?"

"About your age. You're what?"

"Twenty-four."

"She is twenty-five." He grinned, his face reddening.

"Did you tease her a lot?"

"Guest order number 19!"

"That's us!" He ambled to pick up their order.

While he went to get their food, thickness gathered in her throat, her confidence fading. If she wanted to make friends, she needed to keep her resentful feelings under control. She hardly knew Andrew. He seemed like a nice man, except for his arrogance.

"I'm sorry," she said, as he came back with a tray.

He ignored her apologies as he gave her the pancake platter. "Do you have money to rent a car?" He removed the wrapper from his sandwich then closed his eyes. "Lord, thank you breakfast and a new friend to enjoy it with. Amen."

Her stomach hardened. Was that how he ask God to bless the food? At home, her mom would pray, *God, please bless us and bless the food you so abundantly provided.* Where was the blessing in his prayer? Didn't he want God to bless the food? She was not going to say amen to that.

"Hmm?"

"Yes, I could rent a car."

"Good. There is a rental place not far from here." He checked the time on his watch then he finished his sandwich.

Julie found nothing attractive about him. He could be two-faced, and it wore her out. One minute he was gentle. The next, he was a monster. Eric was a pussy cat compared to Andrew. He had better manners even if he didn't talk much. Remembering made her ache.

After breakfast, she left without saying goodbye. As much as she would love to chit chat, he was putting a damper on her spirits. She needed time alone with God.

Joe's Bail4U Bonds, next to Books and Gifts, added weight to her chest. Eric would have posted bail by now. They couldn't keep him in jail for a long time before his trial. If only he would have refused that call, he could've been a free man. Frustration rose in her heart, as she wanted Eric at this moment. She couldn't have him if he was a criminal. She rubbed her palm over her heart before going into the bookstore.

Soft music played in the background, calming Julie's mind and heart. She had gotten off to a rough start, but the thirty minutes of praying, had helped her get the right attitude.

"Good morning! Welcome to Books and Gifts!" A bright young woman with blonde hair stood behind the counter.

Julie put on her best smile and walked with confidence to the counter. "Hi! I'm Julie Henshaw. I am interested in a job."

Her eyes lit up. "Are you from out of town?" She asked, her voice filled with hope.

"Yes. I'm from Montana. You could tell?"

The young woman gave her a disbelieving look. "Yes, but I didn't expect Montana. I need a roommate, but the Lord said she would be coming through these doors. He didn't say when." She smiled.

Little tiny butterflies danced in her stomach. Andrew had mentioned Beth. *That's her name!* He didn't say anything about her needing a roommate. "Are you Beth?"

"That's my name!" She gave an excited smile.

"Andrew told me about you."

Her mouth dropped in surprise. "How do you know Andrew?"

Warmth filled Julie's heart. She spent a good thirty minutes in prayer asking God to give her a right spirit. During her walk, He had reminded her that He had sent Andrew her way, and she needed to show a little more gratitude. He had done a lot more for her than anyone would with that kind of attitude. "He came to my rescue last night. My car died outside your town, and he just happened to drive by."

Beth giggled. "Andrew does not *just happen.* He prays about everything before he *does*. He may be arrogant, but he's good guy and loves God."

The warmth turned to shame as Beth confirmed what God had told her. She had acted a like a spoiled child, wanting to get her way. Was there a way to make it up to him? Maybe if he would let her, she could take him out for lunch. "What kind of foods does Andrew like? I'm just curious."

"Nothing fast food. He likes Asian, Thai, and Greek. He'll eat seafood, chicken, and fish. He isn't a burger lover. Why?"

"Oh nothing. So, can I apply?"

Beth reached under the counter and handed her two pages to fill out. "Do you have work experience?"

"Only as a waitress."

Beth nodded.

###

As Julie exited, Beth's breath bottled up in her heart. If Marilyn hired her, she could get a roommate. Julie seemed like a nice woman. She loved her energy. She would also have someone to worship God with. Her roommate had moved out a month ago and left her to her own devices. Fellowshipping with a Christian roommate was twice as fun as doing it alone.

Julie had gone across to the street to the park. They could picnic there sometime.

Chapter 6

The air chilled as the bells chimed. A man entered the bookstore, browsing among the books. He wore a fedora, but he didn't look frightening.

"Be on Guard."

The man's eyes almost caught Beth's, but she glanced away, not wanting to draw attention. He round the corner, disappearing into the history section of books. *God, is he trouble?*

"Yes."

Beth nodded, keeping an eye on the man.

Marilyn tapped her on her shoulder, causing her to jump. "Are you okay?"

"That man," she whispered. "God says he is dangerous."

"I'll ask him to leave." Marilyn walked over to the history section as he pulled out a book.

The man smiled to Marilyn. "Have you read this book? I've always liked reading about the West." His icy stare froze Beth in her station.

"Can I help you?" Marilyn showed some annoyance in her voice.

"Oh, I'm just looking. Do you like to read history?"

"If you want the book, please make a purchase." Marilyn sounded like he had put her on edge.

"Just looking around. I'll leave." He tipped his hat, and Beth swore he bore his teeth as he left.

Beth let out the tension she had bottled up. "Thank you, Marilyn."

"If he comes back and bothers you, let me know."

"Oh by the way! A possible new applicant walked in before he did." Her mouth dropped as Marilyn gave her a questionable look. "Coincident?"

"We know the people that come here. They are called regulars. Occasionally we have tourists, but not like this morning. Keep your eyes open and ears attentive to God."

"He warned me about him."

Her eyes sparkled. "See?" She went back into her office.

###

As Julie filled out the application, she trembled. Who was watching her? A man had just entered Books and Gifts. Did she know him? He wore a white t-shirt and fedora on his head. He stood taller than Eric. She let out a sigh of relief. *I must be overreacting.* Who would harm her in the daylight? A few minutes later, he had waltzed out. Julie picked up her application and ran to the store. "Who was that?"

"Who was what?" Beth asked.

"The man that just left."

"We don't know, but we sensed he was trouble."

Calm came over her. "You sensed? Are you a Christian?"

Beth smile lit up her eyes. "Yes, ma'am!"

A smile built on her face. "All right!"

"I'm guessing you are too," she said with a hopeful voice.

"Yes, I am. See you later." She ran out to the park.

###

Andrew celebrated all his self-accomplishments. He sold a house Friday, and today he would work escrow. He loved his job. He worked for the best real estate agency in Marysville.

"Have some paperwork for you to do, Andy," his employer addressed him as he laid down the paperwork for another house that was for sale.

He gave a satisfying smile. "Yes, sir!" Another opportunity to prepare a house for sale. And if Julie decided to stay, he could sell her one. She would be so grateful, she would kiss him all over. This made him feel tall, big, and strong. "Yes, sir!" He could sell a house to anyone because he succeeded at that. He put his feet down and tackled the paperwork.

A tall man passed by his office. He looked out of place, and Andrew's breath stalled. Where had he come from? He didn't look like he was from around here. Andrew's scalp prickled. The other night, Julie had shivered. He couldn't figure out why. Yet, seeing this man made even *him* suspicious.

"Lord?" Andrew went into prayer mode.

At lunch time, his skin tingled with surprise as Julie walked in. He didn't expect her to stop by. After what had happened at breakfast, she had given him a feeling that she wanted nothing to do with him.

"What brings you here?" He smiled.

"I wanted to make it up to you, and I won't take no for an answer."

He stared at his computer screen. "You do, huh?"

She glanced around. "Nice office." She smiled to the man getting up. "I bet you sell a lot of houses."

Was she talking to him or Jake? He better play it safe. "We all do. We are successful."

She had an amused smile on her face. "What do you say? No fast food. I promise."

He studied her. Julie didn't look the type to eat Thai food. He had planned on going there with his brother, Nate. He needed to get going to meet him. "I'm going out to have Thai." He narrowed his eyes as he tilted his head.

"Forget it." She walked out.

"Nice going, Andrew." Sarcasm dripped from Jake's mouth. "If you like her, go after her." Jake frowned. "That invitation is for you. Are you trying to keep women away?"

"I got to go!" Andrew stormed out.

As he walked, he looked to heaven. How did his day turn out this way? He felt stressed over little things and blew up. He blew up at Julie, and he blew up Jake. Jake was right. He liked her, and he hated her. Julie seemed to be about self. What she wanted and what she needed. Wasn't he that way too? Didn't he pride himself on helping the helpless? Julie wasn't helpless.

He closed his eyes, *Lord, how can I be her friend, if I mess up every time?* If his father found out, he would give him a disapproving look. He needed to man up. *I should have gotten her phone number.*

"Looks like you could use a ride." Julie's unexpected voice lightened his heart.

"Well, actually, I went for a walk. I'm sorry about earlier."

Her eyes showed understanding. "I've dealt with worse people than you."

He walked to the car. "I lied. I would love to have lunch with you. Do you like Thai?"

"I could give it a try."

"I think you'll enjoy it." He walked with a spring in his step to the passenger side, whistling.

"Show me the way."

"Will do!"

###

As they waited in line, Julie lost her breath. Was this a lunch date? The dark interior gave Julie the impression of an intimate setting. The walls had decorations that hinted of Thailand's culture. What was Thai food like?

Andrew stared in wonder at her. His dreamy green eyes lit up the dark, even glowed like lit candle in a dark room. A smile stretched on his face. "You like what you see?"

"It's different." *Hopefully not too pricey*

"How many in party?" An Asian removed menus from the rack.

"Two," Julie said.

She led them to a table by a window and gave them menus as they sat across from each other.

Andrew was first to hide his face in it, as if he was trying to ignore her.

Eric treated me better than this. Why do I even bother?

The menu had so many strange dishes it made her sick looking at it. *Me and my big mouth. How am I going to eat this? What if I don't like it? And the prices?* She shook her head.

###

Warmth coursed through him. She proved him right. Julie had never had Thai food. The expression on her face was classic. Should he go out of his way and make her feel indebted to him? Or let her squirm? Ah, but he had compassion. "If you can't afford it, I can help you."

"Oh, I can." She offered him a smile. "I'm not a waif, you know."

"Okay. But if you can't, let me know. You wanted to make it up to me, and so I gave you a chance."

"How nice of me." Her voice oozed with sarcasm, but he laughed.

After their meal came, out of impulse, he grabbed her hand. It created a spark and annoyed him. Why? He wasn't interested in her. Even Julie looked surprise but maintained her modesty. He closed his eyes. "Heavenly father, thank you for varieties of food we can eat and try. I pray that we will enjoy in Jesus's name. Amen."

"And bless it too, Jesus," she added.

He nodded tightly.

During the meal, Julie checked her phone several times. Was she in a hurry to leave? She hardly ate anything. "It was your idea," he stated.

"Just feel uneased." She glanced around as if someone was watching.

His eyes flitted to the entrance, but no one had come in. "Earlier, I felt that way, and then I saw a man walk by."

"A man?" Her eyes shot wide

"Yes. I've never seen the likes of him before." He frowned.

Julie shivered. Andrew wanted to put his light coat around her, but he sensed that they needed to leave.

She paid for their meals, then he guided her to the rental, keeping his eye out for anything suspicious. Once inside, he relaxed.

"So you're feeling it too?" Her mouth dropped open.

"Is there anyone in Montana who might want to stalk you?"

"Not that I know of." She shrugged.

"Maybe it's nothing. I should probably get to work. Thanks for lunch."

"Um… you're welcome." Her tone told him she would not eat here again.

Later, a phone call from Books and Gifts removed all worries from Julie's heart. She had spent her afternoon in prayer about this job, and He had given her a sense of calm. If she got this job, she would not owe it to Beth, but to God. She had such confidence that God had led her there. Beth's pleasant personality won her over. She wanted to cherish this moment for ever. Now her burdens lightened. Once Marilyn hired her, she could move in with Beth. They could become best friends. "Hello?"

"Julie Henshaw?" a woman asked

"Yes. Who is this?"

"I'm Marilyn Anderson, the hiring manager from Books and Gifts. How are you?"

"I'm good." She held her breath.

"Great! I went over your application. Are you planning to make Marysville your home?"

"If it works out. I have applied at other places too."

"That's good to keep your options open. Are you available tomorrow at 9:30 a.m.?"

"Yes!"

"Great! Bring a resume, and I will see you tomorrow."

"Okay!" She got off the phone and whooped it up.

Chapter 7

On the day of her interview, Julie's stomach fluttered. Dressed in her white skirt and pink, button-up blouse, she was ready, except for one thing. She only had her boots. They would have to do. She checked to make sure she had not put on too much lipstick and mascara.

"God, I thank you for the opportunity of working in Marysville. Thank you for giving me a second chance. I hope my parents and Eric will forgive me." She prayed for him even though he wasn't a believer. She still cared about him, but after what she had witnessed, she had to leave him and Montana. "Amen."

When she arrived at 8:45 a.m., she wiped her sweaty palms on her skirt and fidgeted with her purse. As she stepped out of the car, she closed her eyes and sighed. She would land this job.

Beth's eyes lit up as she ambled in. "I'll let her know you're here!" She disappeared into the back room.

Julie smiled. She loved her enthusiasm. "Okay."

Soon after that, Beth came out into the front. "Go right in. Straight down and to the right. Her door is open."

As Julie walked in, a woman wearing a black sweater over a red camisole stood up to greet her. "Hello, Julie. I'm Marilyn Anderson." She extended her hand. "Have a seat."

Julie shook her head and sat in a plastic chair in front of the desk. "Thanks for taking your time today." Julie smiled.

"I had my doubts. Can I see your resume?"

Julie handed it to her, giving her a confident smile.

"You have worked as a waitress at Julz and Jayz for six years?"

"Yes."

"What was that like?"

"They keep me busy. I had a few customers that would flirt with me and some that enjoy my presence."

"Is there a reason why you left Montana?"

Julie shrugged. "I've lived there all my life. It was time for a change." She forced a smile.

"And you think you'll like it here?"

"I don't see why not?"

"Working in a bookstore is not the same as working as a waitress. You'll be stacking books, shelving, pricing, and assisting customers..." She smiled as Julie nodded at every job duty. "Okay. I'll call your references and see what they will say. I have other applicants, so continue to keep your options open." She saw her to the door.

As Julie left, she put on a smile for Beth.

Beth frowned. "It didn't go well?"

"It's in God's hands. Don't give up." Julie reached in her purse and gave her a piece of paper with her number on it. "I'd like us to be friends."

Beth gasped. "Yes! Just a minute." She ran to the backroom and came back with a business card. "Number on back." She smile wide as they exchanged numbers.

###

Andrew leaned back in his chair, and closed his eyes. His day had started out rough. Five blocks from his house, his engine died. He wasn't sure he would get to work in time, and his employer, Marvin Hassell, didn't look kindly on tardiness. However, Nate had come along and given him a ride to work. Later, he would have to get his car fixed. Did Julie get hers fixed? His situation put him in her place. Imagine being a woman and not knowing how to fix a car. His car just needed a new battery.

Yesterday, she was at the park praying. Thickness had gathered in his throat. In spite of her selfishness, her beauty radiated like the sun. Why couldn't that be more evident in her life? What was she praying about? Him? He didn't blame her. He purposefully chose that restaurant to see what kind of reaction she would have. He regretted it. A tear strayed down his cheeks. *Help me, be a better man, God.*

His supervisor put paperwork on his desk. "Time to get to work, Andrew."

"Yes, sir." He began working on the escrow.

Just before lunch time, the office chilled. Was someone watching him? Why? He twisted at his dress shirt just as that same man walked past his office. Andrew jumped up and bolted to the door. "Hey you!"

The man turned and smiled. "Yes?"

"Do I know you?"

The man's eyes darkened. "Maybe. Maybe not." He grinned. "Have a good day!" He laughed as he walked away.

Andrew chased after him. "I'm not done talking to you." He grabbed him and turned him around. The man stood three inches taller than Andrew, but with bold determination, he said, "Stay away from my friends!" He raised his fist.

"You're no match for me!" By his sheer strength, the man pushed Andrew and hurled him to wall, causing him to fall. He laughed as he walked away.

"And you're no match for God either!" He got up and stormed to his office. He needed to cool down before he grabbed a bite to eat.

###

A black, leather-bound, compact book sat on top of the stand. Should she read it? Her parents raised her to always read the Bible and pray. Would she find her answers? Maybe she could ask Beth. Was she still working? She loved Beth's personality. She needed friends like that. She'd give her a call. She fumbled in her purse for the card Beth had given her then punched the numbers in the keypad.

"Hello?"

"Hi, Beth. This is Julie."

"Oh, hi! I was just signing out from work. Want to grab a bite to eat?"

Beth's invitation gave her the jolt she needed. "Yes! Yes! Let's do! I need a friend right now."

"Do you like Asian food?"

"As long as it's not Thai." She wrinkled her nose.

"You don't like Thai?" Beth sounded shocked. "Why not?"

"Bad experience is all I could say."

"Well, you'll like Chinese. I'll pick you up in ten minutes."

"I look forward to it." She ended the call.

A warm tingling pulsed through her legs. God had overwhelmed her with his goodness. "Thank you for Beth, Jesus!" Did Beth have some good news? She hoped so. Of course, it would take time to get a job. What did she expect? A woman from the North wanting a job? God would work it out.

A knock on the door alerted Julie. "It's me! Beth!"

"I'm coming!" She picked up her purse and walked out.

Beth's tall and not so lean body took her breath away. Julie had only seen her chest and up at the bookstore. She looked great! "Do you have a boyfriend? Just curious."

"I see him from time to time." She led her out to a Volkswagen car.

Julie gasped. "Those cars are so cute! I have a jeep."

"Jeeps are nice. The door is unlocked."

Julie's mouth dropped open as Beth climbed into her little car. She did it with such grace. Julie followed suit and managed to fit in.

Soft instrumental music played on her radio. Julie's breath hitched. The music intrigued her. Where she came from, she listened to hymns or country music. Singers like Reba McIntyre and Rascal Flatts. "What is that you are listening to?" She had heard it in the store too.

"Soft Christian inspirational music. Marilyn introduced it to me." She began the drive.

"Your employer?" Her eyes widened

Beth smiled wide. "Yes, ma'am. I didn't know until my first day, and I asked her about it."

"How long have you worked there?" She leaned forward.

"Seven years." Beth's mouth curved into a smile.

"Did you grow up here?"

"Yes, ma'am! Anymore questions?" She giggled.

"I hear a woman singing. How is it instrumental?"

"Some are and some aren't, but the words help."

###

Driving down the road, Beth felt alive. She had high hopes that Marilyn would hire Julie. Before she left work, she had asked if she would consider hiring Julie. Marilyn had given no indication she would. However, Beth had peace in her heart and that sufficed her. "I hope you can make Marysville your home! It has so much to offer. I am so glad you're a Christian! How long have you known Jesus?"

"Since I was six."

"Wow! And you are how old?" Her mouth dropped open.

"Twenty-four. I know, I'm young."

"I'm twenty-six. Nice to meet you."

"You too!"

"So have you eaten Chinese or Japanese food?"

"No."

"No? Where are you from again?"

"Montana."

"They don't have Asian food over there?"

"What have you not tried?" Julie stared at her, wanting to challenge her.

"Mexican. I don't like beans, and the spices upset my stomach."

Julie scrunched her eyes in confusion. "If you never tried it, how would you know?"

"My boyfriend gave me a bite of his burrito." Beth answered, and Julie frowned. "So do you have someone special in your life? Andrew said he rescued you."

"No. I recently broke up with my boyfriend." She squirmed in her seat, staring out the window. "I have a question."

"Okay."

"Do you play the same music in the store? I would think it would put customers to sleep?" She regarded her.

"Although it's a secular book store, Marilyn believes if you play soothing music, the people will stay."

Julie smiled. "I see."

Beth arrived at Chinese Garden. She jumped out of the car as her heart pounded. She couldn't wait to see how Julie would like Chinese food. "What do you think?"

Julie glanced around and nodded. "Not bad."

Beth smiled. "Tell me about Eric."

Julie giggled. "My parents are funny. Eric is five years older than me, and yet my mother loved him." She stared at the floor.

Beth picked up on a cue. Julie hadn't fallen in love with Eric! Her parents had. "Julie, did you date Eric because of your parents?"

"Sort of. I mean, he seemed really nice, and I was still young. I turned twenty-two four months before I met him. My parents liked him because he was a rancher's son. They liked the idea of me dating one too."

"Did you date to make them happy?"

"At first. Also, I settled for him because there was no one else."

"Now I understand! Oh, Julie!"

Chapter 8

They were waiting in line when the door swung open. Julie hid her smile as Andrew walked in, glancing behind himself. He was out of breath. The hair on her arms and neck lifted. Did something happen?

Beth looked his direction. "Hi, Andrew!" She smiled.

"Hey, Beth." His eyes lit up. "Julie! I'm glad to see you. I saw him."

"Who?"

"That man that gave you the chills. He didn't tell me his name."

Julie ground her teeth. She wished God would make him go away. Why couldn't he leave her alone? Ever since she arrived in California, he had followed her. "I hope you gave him a piece of your mind." Her lips flattened.

"Oh, I did. He said 'you're no match for me,' then he walked away."

Beth gasped. "You too?"

Julie's stomach clenched. Why was this man bothering them? She had never seen him, but she had sensed a dark presence that brought her chills. "Andrew that must be why I was shivering when you looked at my car. You said you weren't cold."

"I wasn't. I guess...I was...too high on myself to notice." He looked down.

"So you did rescue her?" Beth asked in surprise. "How sweet."

Andrew blushed. "Just making my old man proud."

"Julie, he's Nate's brother too." Beth smiled widely.

"He told me about his siblings."

"Are you alone, Andrew?" Beth asked

"Kelly will be joining me soon."

Julie felt her heart sink into her stomach. Andrew had a girlfriend. Why did she ever think a handsome man like him wouldn't have a girlfriend?

"Kelly is his sister," Beth said.

Julie's heart took flight. She might just have a chance.

A Chinese waitress greeted them. "How many in party?" Her almond shaped eyes looked at them.

"Two," Beth said.

Julie and Beth followed the waitress, but she cast secret glances at Andrew.

"What do you think?" Beth asked as the waitress seated them

Julie's heart hammered. Andrew looked rather dashing in his white dress shirt and gray khakis. If only he wasn't so arrogant. It blessed her heart when Beth confirmed that he was a Christian. God could be working on his heart as He was on hers.

Beth must have read her mind. "Before you date again, make sure he is what the Lord has for you. Andrew had a girlfriend that led him on. It took him two years to get over it."

Julie said nothing.

###

Kelly waved him over as he neared her table. "Andrew, did you hurt yourself?" Kelly asked, pointing to the bandage on his forehead

That jerk made him heat up. He had no right to stalk Julie. What had she done to deserve such treatment? Was he the one that caused her timing belt to malfunction? He would love tell him off! That low-life needed to get a job!

"Wow! You're steamed. You better cool it." Kelly gasped

"This man comes to town and gives everyone a bad vibe! I don't get it!" He crossed his arms.

She gasped. "Everyone? Or just you?"

"Julie, Beth, and me."

"Ju—that woman by Beth? Would you like to invite her over? I've never seen you get hot over a woman," she teased.

"It's not funny, Kel. She couldn't enjoy her lunch because of him. He is all riddles too." He went into mocking mode "Maybe. Maybe not!" he muttered, shaking his head. "What a jerk."

"She's coming this way… Hi!"

Julie stood there looking concerned. "What happened to you?"

"Nothing really."

She smiled at Kelly. "Hi! You must be Andrew's sister. I wish I had one." She sat down by Kelly. "I'm Julie."

"Sorry you don't have one. Be blessed you don't have bratty brothers."

Andrew rolled his eyes. "Bratty? We've been good to you."

"Don't let his charisma fool you. It's all an act," Kelly teased.

He gasped. "It's not an act! I do have charisma!"

Julie giggled. "He's funny when he's red."

"Yeah. I love my brothers. They spoil me." She ruffled his hair.

"Well, off to the ladies' room." Julie got up and headed toward the back.

His heart played like a melody on a piano. As she walked away, she created quite a breeze, causing the hair on his arm to stand on end. He wanted an excuse to go see her. "Excuse me." He scooted out and headed toward the men's room.

###

Andrew's presence made her worries fall away. He overwhelmed her when he told his sister what happened. He fought for her! Would Eric fight for her the same way he did? He made her feel good! She wanted the feeling to last. As she walked out, she walked into him, but she embraced him. "Thank you!"

His face flushed. "For what?"

"Coming to my defense. Tell me, what did he look like?"

"Ugly as hell. You're welcome." A smile danced on his lips.

Her chest fluttered. His green eyes shone and softened, and his scent was mild and pleasing. She loved his lopsided smile.

"What are you staring at?"

"You." She lowered her voice.

He gave her a lopsided grin. "You're not too bad looking yourself. Where did you say you were from?"

"Montana."

"And you come here because...?" He pulled away when she touched his face. "Um..."

"What?"

"People watching."

"So?"

"Time to eat." He walked past her.

Julie shook her head as she returned to her seat.

###

After the waitress took their orders, Beth considered her words. "I see you're attracted to Andrew. Do you have feelings for him? Or are you playing with his heart?"

"Yes, of course I have feelings for him! Or he wouldn't get under my skin so much!" she said rather quickly.

"So you are over Eric?"

"Yes!"

"It takes a while to get over someone," she said, and Julie shrugged. "You were twenty when you met him?"

"Twenty-two." She sighed heavily as Beth gave her a concerned look.

"And he hasn't asked you to marry him?"

She gave a sad nod. "I wanted him to. I waited, but it never happened."

"Maybe he was not ready for marriage. What do you know about him?" She took a sip of her tea.

"He's not very communicative, which is what drew me to him. I loved his quiet nature. I only knew about his abuse."

"Oh, Julie!"

"My mother thinks I'm a horrible person for turning Eric in. I haven't the heart to call her."

Julie's plight weighed heavily on her heart. "I'm sorry, Julie. That must be hard."

Julie nodded. "I just can't go back to Montana. To everything." Tears streaked her face.

"Also, I have to be honest. Marilyn did have other applicants. Not long ago, she hired a man who used the store as a means to get a woman. He even hit on me. She wants someone who plans to stay."

"She gave me the impression she wasn't going to hire me either." Her voice went flat.

"But don't give up hope. If this is where God has you, then you will get the job. Sunday is in five days. Would you like to come to church with me?"

Julie smiled. "I would love to."

"Awesome."

###

Julie waited in the lobby while Beth paid for their lunch. Praise filled her heart, and tears of joy escaped her eyes. She didn't deserved anyone's friendship, but all of them accepted her unconditionally.

Andrew lined up behind Beth, but Kelly walked over to Julie. There was so much love and acceptance in her eyes. "He really likes you. He won't admit it, but he does. I hope he doesn't turn you off." His defense of her had made her head spin. Had Eric ever had that effect on her? He had never fought for her. If anyone thought Andrew would turn her away, she would show them just how much she cared.

Lord, help me be less selfish and more like you.

Beth's words rang in her mind: *make sure he is the one.*

As they walked to Beth's car, the hair on the back of Beth's neck lifted. She fumbled for her keys and rushed to unlock her door. "Get in!" She urged as Julie glanced around, shivering. Julie did, and Beth followed suit. "I'm not paranoid, but I swore someone was watching us. Julie, what do you know about Eric? Does he have enemies?" She pulled out and drove Julie back to her motel.

Her eyes darted everywhere. "Is Andrew going back to work?"

"He has."

Julie stared at the window. "I don't know if Eric has enemies. I've been sheltered, so I have little to say about him."

"In the two years you've dated him, you never met any, or he hasn't talked about any?"

"When we date, he usually talks about ranching. I asked him about his upbringing, and he just said that his father abused him."

"Is his father still alive?"

"Both his parents are dead. He just has a brother."

Beth's heart hurt for Eric. Julie must have been a drop of sunshine for him. "Does he know Jesus?"

She shook her head. "He's miserable. He needs Him." As Beth said that, her breath bottled up. God had allowed Julie to come here so they both could heal. They needed to pray for Eric. Was it possible God would reunite the two? Her only concern was whether Julie and Andrew would be friends. She would hate to see Julie break his heart.

Julie nodded. "Yes he does." Her voice softened.

Beth arrived at Julie's motel. "If you don't feel safe, call upon Jesus. He's your shelter and your safe refuge. Have you ever thought about confessing Psalms 91?"

Julie shot her a look. "Psalms 91? No."

"David wrote that by staying continually in God's presence, that no harm or evil can come near you. But you must stay in it. Read it and study it." She smiled.

Julie nodded in agreement then reached to hug Beth. "Thanks for being a friend."

"Aww, you're welcome. I sure hope Marilyn hires you."

"Me too." She stepped out.

###

That night, as Julie spent time in prayer, the air chilled. Julie's ears perked up to any outside sounds, but all was quiet. Too quiet. She walked to the window. A woman closed her car door, followed by a man stepping out and leading her to the motel. Across the street, a woman walked her German shepard, but no lone man. *Must be my imagination.*

Julie returned to her time in prayer.

A few minutes later, an unexpected knock startled her.

"Don't answer."

Julie slowed her breath. It was that man. Why would Jesus warn her not to answer?

"Flower delivery!" a young male voice answered.

###

"What's taking him long?" Drew muttered under his breath. He had left to deliver the flowers ten minutes ago! Julie should have accepted them by now. Maybe he should have had the note read "From lover boy." He cackled. His words caught in his throat. Why hadn't he thought about that? If Eric found out that Julie had moved on, it would destroy him. Ahh, but he wanted her for himself. And his day would come.

The delivery boy had returned with the flowers and the note. Drew lips pressed in straight line. "She won't accept them. I even told him they were from her new friend. She won't even answer the door."

His stomach clenched. What woman would not want flowers? "Did you tell her they were yellow?" He shook his head, and Drew's heart rate went up. "You should have. They are her favorite." He prided himself on that knowledge. "Thanks for trying." He took the flowers and put them in the seat.

The next time, he would succeed.

Chapter 9

Sunday morning came, and butterflies fluttered about. Julie took her yellow dress with a white belt out of her garment bag. Would Andrew be at church? Ever since his confession, he had put a song in her heart. She just needed to pray and ask God to change both of them. They both had issues. What were his issues?

After she dressed, she adorned her neck with a cross necklace her mother had given her for her last birthday. She pressed it to her neck. She loved her mother, but after their last phone call, she didn't want to hear from her again.

You owe him the truth. Beth's words came at her, and it gave her a headache. Eric was behind bars. What good would it do to tell him to his face? She had told him on the phone, hadn't she?

Beth had given her the address, as she wanted Julie to take her own car and pray. She paid the mechanic, and her car was ready the day before. She appreciated Beth's words of advice cautioning her to not break Andrew's heart, but he was a big boy. He could handle himself.

The little white church sat on the corner of Fifth Avenue and Lakeview Road. She parked in the parking lot behind the church, not too far from Beth's yellow bug.

Beth waved to Julie as she neared the sanctuary. "Over here!"

"Hi!" She followed Beth into the lobby where members greeted her.

"Alyssa, meet Julie. She is new in town. Julie, Alyssa."

Alyssa was in her forties. She was a little plump, but was about Beth's height. She wore her brown hair in a bun. "Hi, Julie. Nice to meet you." She offered her hand to shake.

"Likewise." She accepted the handshake.

As they went out into the sanctuary, Beth scanned the room then smiled. She led Julie to a pew behind the brothers.

Andrew's eyes met hers, and her heart fluttered. He had the kindest green eyes she had ever seen. "Glad you came, Julie."

"I'm glad too." She sat behind him then opened her bulletin.

"Julie, this is my man Nate. Nate, Julie."

"Andrew told me about you. Nice to meet you."

Did Julie blush? She felt she did. "Nice to meet you too." She shook his hand.

Andrew chuckled.

As the sermon began, Julie forgot to breathe. The pastor preached on The Holy Spirit and how he was a part of every Christian's life and not just one third of the trinity. This teaching was new to her. All her life, He had only been in her heart has the seal of her salvation. His sermon intrigued her.

"In Isaiah it says, 'You will hear a voice behind you saying, this is the way. Walk in it...' "

Julie gulped. Had she listened to the Holy Spirit? Did he tell her to come to California? She thought she had, but now she questioned it. Was it her own idea? Beth put a comforting hand on her back. "I haven't been that close to God because of Eric. Maybe I need to draw close to Him first."

"That's a great idea! Pray in the Spirit too."

"Pray in the spirit?"

"Yes. You pray in words that only the Holy Spirit understands." She demonstrated, and Julie gave her a confused look. "Start with a few syllables."

"If you have not received Jesus in your heart," the pastor concluded, "and you would like the Holy Spirit working in you, please come forward at the end of the service. I would be glad to talk to you. God bless, and you all have a good day."

###

Andrew's heart hammered. "I was wondering if you would like to have lunch by the river," he whispered in her ear.

Julie glanced at Beth who had a beaming expression on her face. She relaxed. "Why don't we make it like a double date?" Her eyes sparkled.

"That's a great idea! Let's leave them alone," Beth said.

"Are you sure?" Nate asked.

"Positive. See you two there." Beth led Nate out of the sanctuary.

Andrew's pulse raced. What a beautiful fall day. The blue sky, colorful leaves in a tree, and a beautiful woman to enjoy a picnic with made it just right. "Seems like forever since we last seen each other."

Julie smiled, glancing around, but she fixed her eyes on him. "Has it?"

"Did you get a job yet?"

She frowned. "No. I have applied at every place imaginable."

"Beth said you used to wait tables. Have you thought about doing that again?"

"I waited tables because it was the only thing in Montana to do. I like Books and Gifts."

"I was hoping that we could picnic as...a date. I really like you."

Julie's eyes shone. "I like you too."

He had a silly grin on his face. "How would you feel riding in a car with me?"

"I think I should go in my own."

"Okay. We better get going. Don't worry about bringing something."

"I won't."

He kissed her cheeks then whistled as he walked to his car

###

As Julie ambled to her car, the hair on the back of her neck stood on end. Was that man back? Beth stood by her car waving at her, and Andrew climbed into his BMW. The parking lot had a few cars parked in it. The pastor smiled and whistled as he locked up the church. *Must be my imagination.* She kept her eye on her surroundings as she climbed into her car. Julie checked the time on her cell phone.

Beth rushed to her car. "Do you need a ride to the lake?"

Julie looked up. "I can follow you."

"I noticed you were looking around."

"I thought the man was watching me."

Beth squinted as she glanced around. She covered her mouth as if she noticed something. "I'll be back." Beth ran off.

Lord did he follow me? Ever since Julie shared what was on her heart, Beth relaxed and was more for her dating Andrew. A feeling of warmth came over as she touched where he had kissed her. *Oh God, please make this work.* So why did she feel as if they had released Eric and he was after her? *How absurd!*

Beth returned, out of breath. "I saw a black Corvette parking a few blocks away, but it was gone when I got there. Maybe someone looking for a street."

"Could be."

"I'm going to stop by the store to buy a few things for the picnic. Do you mind?"

Andrew had the dreamiest of green eyes, and she loved how his smile tugged at the corner of his lips. She gave a happy sigh. Andrew made her feel safe and accepted. He made her feel...loved. She had only seen him a couple of times. She needed a real date with him. "You okay with Andrew and me?"

"As long as you have peace that he's the one for you. I would love for you two to know each other."

Julie smiled. She would love it too. "Okay."

Beth ambled to her car. "Do you want to follow me? I need to stop by my apartment."

"I'll follow you."

Beth smiled wide then climbed in her car.

As Julie followed Beth, she worshipped God in her heart. Her breath quickened. God had been so good! Ever since she came to California, he had given her new friends with the kind of people she wanted to imitate. She didn't long for marriage with Eric. She hardly knew the man. She had dated him because her parents approved of him. God had saved her from disappointment. What if he hadn't accepted the call? She had been prepared for a proposal. Either way she would have ended up making the biggest mistake of her life and have an unhappy marriage, or he would disappoint her. God had given her a desire to come to California. He had led her straight to Beth. What Julie longed for was a closer walk with God. Tears filled her eyes as she practiced praying in the spirit.

####

Picnicking with her new friends gave Julie a sense of calm. Last night she had nightmares that sent a coldness to the core of her body. Andrew and Julie had shared a kiss then he fell down dead. She had prayed and asked God to give her peace.

"Would you like to walk with me?" Andrew broke her train of thought.

She tingled with excitement. They could share their feelings without people around. Recently she found out he liked her. Was he going to ask her to go steady with him? Would he hold her hand? Last time, it created a spark. She just hoped her stalker wouldn't be around. She couldn't enjoy her meal at the Thai restaurant. "Sure!"

He held his hand out for her, and she grabbed it; her fingers tingled. She gave him a smile as he helped her out.

As they walked, his eyes shone like the sun, and he breathed in and out. "About last night. I'm sorry I worried you." Someone tried to deliver flowers and she thought they were from him. She had called Andrew in her worried state. He raised a false alarm, thinking it was from her stalker. Andrew wouldn't know her favorite flowers were.

"I forgive you."

"I guess that... I care about you." His eyes met hers. "I've never met... anyone like you... How do you feel about me?"

"You make all my worries go away." She covered her mouth. "I shouldn't have said that. This morning, I had peace in my heart, after I gave God my worries. Last night I was about to read about abiding in God's presence because I felt unsafe. The flowers distracted me, but I let my selfishness get in the way. I told Beth, and she said the devil tried to distract me. I got angry."

"So it was what I thought."

"What?"

"He tried with me too. Got me anxious so I reacted." His face reddened.

He left her breathless. Andrew shared the same concern she did. Did he pray in the spirit? She had forgotten to do that. Andrew always seemed to come to her rescue. Like they were connected. What was he like before she met him? The night her car died, he had shown himself a hero. He even fought for her, and it melted her heart. He liked her? Was he falling for her?

"I appreciate you." She softened her tone.

Her hand moistened as he held it. "Are you enjoying the walk?"

"I enjoy being with you."

His eyes danced. "Me too. I wish I knew why." He laughed.

###

As they stopped by a tree, his heart played a melody. He leaned in, wanting to get close to her. He would fight again for her if he needed to, and he would let her go if she chose to return home to Montana. He wanted to live for the moment. "Don't worry about what Beth and Kelly said about me. My ex-girlfriend broke up with me two years ago. I'm over that just as you are over your previous boyfriend."

A slow smile tugged at the corner of her lips. "Okay."

His fingers found a way to her face, and she didn't flinch. "Would you consider going out me again? Next time we will go where you would like to go."

Her cell phone ruined the moment as she pressed her lips together. "My mom."

"I'll wait."

"What is it, Mom…? You saw him at church? Since when...? Well, it may not last... I don't know, Mom..."

From Julie's end, it sounded like Eric was out of jail, and Julie wasn't ready to see him. He had hesitated to ask her on a date, but he had peace.

Julie gave a heavy sigh. "Of all times!"

"What's wrong?" He lifted her downcast face. He wanted to lift her spirits.

"Mom saw Eric in church today. He's out on bail." She shivered.

###

Meanwhile in Montana, joy filled Eric's heart. Randy had bailed him out, and now he could go back to ranching. Yet his insides shook as he castrated one of his cows. With Julie out of his protection, Drew could find her, and God knows what kind of evil he would do to her. He closed his eyes. "Lord, I thank you for a second chance to make things right. Please keep Julie safe. Amen." He took out his cell phone. Would Julie have the same number? Should he call her? He shook his head. He had no peace.

While in jail, his fellow prisoners scoffed when the prison guard had released him yet he gave them to the Lord. He made it his mission to pray for them. Eric felt the need to do so now. He had studied Paul's life and wanted to imitate him. He took the small bible out of his pocket and looked for one of the Pauline letters to the Philippians.

"Be anxious for nothing, but in *everything, by prayer and supplication,* with *thanksgiving, let your requests be made known to God..."*

Goosebumps slid across his back. Those two words removed all his worries. He sensed a presence so great he fell down in worship. He wanted Randy and John to experience this, but they were doing what he should be doing. What was he supposed to do?

Moo

A grin spread across his face. Of course. Eric remained in prayer as he attended to the cow.

Chapter 10

The news of Eric's release tightened around Andrew's heart. Eric didn't deserve her. Going to church does not make one a Christian. If Eric came here, come rain or sun, he would prove his worth once and for all.

After he cooled off, they continued to walk. He wanted to know about Julie. "So you were born in Montana?"

"Born and raised. We lived in Helena for a few years until I was ten, then my dad's boss transferred him to Bozeman. Montana is known as the Big Sky State. We have lots of mountains and farming and ranching communities...."

"Do you miss Montana?" His eyes probed hers. "Do you miss home?"

"I try not to." She gave him a faint smile. "I had a job that kept me busy, but I never found the person I wanted to marry. When I did, he was already taken."

"Who was that?"

"My pastor."

"Eric took you away from Jesus?"

"As long as I dated him, I acted like a person of the world. I wanted to please him. I'm so grateful that God kept him from proposing to me."

His eyes sparkled. "I've been praying for you. I don't know if Beth told you, but my last girlfriend found another man, and we had dated each other for six months. I was deeply in love with her."

"Yes, Beth told me. This is why I want to take it slow. Is that okay?"

"I am more than okay with that. I have a question. Would you consider having dinner with me Friday night?"

###

Friday night? What if she couldn't stay in the motel? She still needed a job and a place to live. She couldn't make any promises. She bit her lips. "Umm..."

Andrew frowned. "What's wrong?"

"Let's see what happens. I have been here five days and still no job. What if I go homeless? Or worse yet, go home because it didn't work out here?"

"If you have faith, it will work out. Trust God."

"I will."

They came to an oak tree, and Andrew stopped her. She lost herself in his sea of green. Her heart banged, and her breath quickened. He was going to kiss her. She would let him. Her lips parted. Her eyes closed.

"There you are!" Beth's announcement ruined the moment.

Andrew backed away. "Sorry." His face reddened. "I guess I got lost in you."

"I did too."

"You two have been gone a half hour. We were concerned."

They would have to kiss another time. She would have loved to have kissed him, but it was too early. Beth had come at a good time even if Julie's flesh wanted it. "Thanks, Beth."

"Yes. Thank you." Even Andrew sounded disappointed, but he managed it well.

They followed Beth to the picnic area. "If you two want to stay, it's up to you. Nate noticed a black Corvette hanging around."

Julie quickened her breath. "The same one you saw earlier?"

"Not sure, it could be. He wrote down the license plate. He is going to find out who it belongs to."

Andrew gave her a concerned look. "Do you feel like going back to the motel?"

She would love if she could stay with Andrew. She didn't want to go back to a lonely room. She could visit with Beth. Did Beth have plans?

Beth gazed into Nate's eyes, but their lips had not touched. What kind of relationship did she have with him? They dated for a year? Her adrenaline jumped. Was he about to propose to her?

"He loves her." Andrew broke her thoughts.

"Has he proposed to her?"

"Nate has a fear of commitment. He has dated Beth off and on."

"She sees him from time to time, right?"

He nodded.

Was Andrew the same way? He admitted that his last girlfriend had broken up with him after six months. Was Eric the same way? They dated for two years, but he never proposed. She wanted someone to grow old with and have many children. Did she want that with Andrew? She touched her heart.

###

Watching the lovers have a picnic, Drew took out his cell phone and took a couple of photos of Julie and her lover having a picnic. "How sweet," he mocked.

Lydia was in the front seat, watching with him. "He doesn't seem her type."

"You know who her type is, don't you?" A malicious grin was on his face.

"You are, of course."

"She didn't accept the flowers, but I'll try a box of dark chocolates."

Julie had gotten up and taken hold of that loser's hand. His breathing became heavier. "He's not right for her, and I need to show him that." He touched Lydia's face. "Do me a favor. Throw this rock at his house." He gave her a round, jagged rock about 6 inches in diameter.

She stared in disbelief at the rock. "Why?" Her mouth fell open.

"As a warning. I love getting him riled up."

A smile played on her lips. "Anything for you."

###

Andrew drove, and Julie followed him to his house. It wasn't the tidiest of houses, but it was home. He enjoyed the picnic, but as he neared his house, anger filled his heart. The glass on his left window had a hole and cracks as if someone had thrown a rock. *Whoever smashed my window will pay!*

Julie stepped out and gasped. "I can't believe it!"

Andrew reached a boiling point. "You want to guess who?" he shouted. He took out his cell phone and called the police.

"Marysville Police Department. Sergeant Richardson speaking. How can I help you?"

"I would like to report a crime. Some bozo smashed my window of my house." He tried to control his tone. Julie was walking toward his house." Julie, don't touch anything!"

"And who is calling?"

"Andrew Slayton. I live at 3115 North Juniper Way."

The officer sounded as if he was typing something. "I'll send a couple officers down there."

"Thanks." He hung up then rushed to Julie. "Are you okay?"

Julie blanched. "Do you think—Beth said she saw a black Corvette."

Julie's suspicion tightened his heart. He wouldn't put it past that bastard to have thrown a rock at his house. Was it a warning? Last night, he had thought the secret admirer was that man they had all seen, except Julie. And he wanted to protect her. Whoever threw that rock would pay dearly. "The same one who sent you the flowers."

She gasped. "No!"

"Beth saw his car at the park—I mean ever since you arrived it is as if he followed you."

Julie looked away. "I'm sorry. I didn't know."

Love filled his heart as he turned her to him. "Don't be sorry, Julie. I don't blame you and neither does God."

###

As the police arrived, Andrew left to go talk to the police, and Julie tensed up. How could this happen to Andrew? Why? The other day Andrew had had a confrontation with him. Was that why? Julie walked to her car and waited inside. They needed her help. She would just pray.

The investigator walked to the house and glanced around. He opened the door and walked in. Andrew must have given him the key. She lost her breath as he came out. He held a rock as big as his hand.

The other officer nodded, and they bagged the rock.

Andrew walked to her car and poked his head in. "The police suggest I find another place to stay for a while until they catch him."

"They think he will do it again?"

"Just for safety measures. I'm going to call Nate. Sorry you had to see this."

Her heart pounded. "I hope they catch him!" She scowled.

"Same here." He pulled his head out and made a call on his phone. "Hey, Nate, your brother here. Some bozo threw a rock at my window..." Minutes later he smiled as he got off the phone. "Andrew is okay with me coming over. And he suggest you stay with Beth for a while. I told the police about the flowers. They didn't seem concerned, but I am."

Her throat constricted. Who did Nate think he was? She could take care of herself! Beth told her if she felt unsafe to abide in God's presence. And she would. "Regardless of what Nate thinks, I'm going back to the motel."

"Suit yourself. You want me to follow you?"

His offer to follow her warmed her heart. He must want to make sure she was safe. "Yes, please."

"Let me see if they needed anything more from me than we will go."

"Okay."

He approached the officers. As she watched, her breath hitched. He was leading them to her car. Did they have questions for her?

"Miss Henshaw, I am officer Davenport. Can you tell us anything to help us? Andrew said this guy may have followed you here."

"I don't know who he is. Sorry."

"Your friend said you were with him when it happened?"

"We were on a picnic, yes."

"Did you see anything suspicious?"

"No, my friend Beth has."

"Okay. We have her name down. If you know anything, give us a call."

"I will."

The officer nodded to Andrew and headed to the patrol c

Chapter 11

Frustration set in as day after day, no employer gave Julie any hope of having a job. Her phone sat on the stand. Silent. Julie's hope faded away. She didn't want to work as a waitress, but it might be her only option. She gave a heavy sigh. "Jesus, I thought it was your will for me to come here, but no one will hire me. Now what?"

Trouble also seemed to follow her. Ever since she came into town, someone had followed her and threatened to harm her friends. They had found out the prints on the rock belonged to a woman and not to that man. It didn't make her life easier.

So what could she do? She still had money in her bank, but she hadn't saved enough to plan for her future. Would it be a good idea to earn a degree? Now she had to. It was either live on the streets, which was beneath her, or go home. Did she really want to face everyone she had let down?

"Fall afresh on me, Holy Spirit." As soon as she prayed, the Holy Spirit came upon her and gave her the utterance to pray in tongues. Her mouth parted. "Wow." She continued to pray.

It was during this time, as she fell into a trance, her breath quickened. An image of a man on a horse galloped toward her. It took place at night, and she couldn't make out that man. He couldn't be Eric. Or was he? Was Eric coming for her? Had her past come to hunt her?

"Be on guard. The devil is prowling around like a lion."

The air chilled. The man was back? Was he in the motel? Who else besides the devil would wish her harm? Was that why she felt uneasy? Beth said there was a black Corvette that waited around, but not a horse. Unless the horse...represented a...black...car. Was he here now?

Her cell phone rang and she jumped. "Hello?"

"Julie, come stay with me for a while." Beth's voice took on concern.

"Are you sensing something?"

"Yes. Just pack quickly and come here. I live at 300 Park Street."

Her lungs expanded. Beth had sensed danger just as she had. If God hadn't quickened her to use her spirit language, He might not have given her that vision before Beth confirmed it.

She got off the phone and wasted no time packing her suitcase. "Thank you, God." She locked up as she rushed out of her room.

As she arrived, Beth had a worried expression on her face. "I saw the same black car, and it had a Montana license plate. God quickened me to call you."

Julie's words lodged in her throat. Montana? Who did she know drove a black Corvette? Eric drove a dark gray Ford pickup truck. It didn't make any sense. Randy drove a white truck and John a green one. In Montana, she didn't feel in danger. Should she go home? She shook her head. "Are you sure it wasn't a truck?"

"I'm certain it was a Corvette." Beth opened the door for her. "I'm convinced it's the same man."

Julie's eyes widened. "Weird."

"Have you read Psalms 91?"

"Yes. Finally!"

"I'm so relieved," She let out a breath. "I have a spare bed. God told me to let you stay the rest of the week."

"I appreciate that, Beth Thank you." Julie sat on the bed and took out the Bible.

Beth's phone rang. "Hello...Hi...You are?" Beth glanced at her. "Okay. I'll tell her. See you tomorrow." She hit end call. "That was Marilyn. Something came up, and she has to leave Marysville, so her assistant is taking over." Hope was in her eyes. This could be good. She grinned.

"Who is her assistant?"

"Victoria Edwards." She entered the next room.

###

That night, butterflies danced in Julie's stomach. Would she be able to enjoy her date without someone stalking her? She had abided in God's presence, allowing him to secure her and keep harm away from her. If she stayed in His will, then he would protect her. She couldn't wait to spend alone time with Andrew. It would be the first time he invited her on a date...without Beth and Nate.

Julie opened her garment bag. She had a long white dress with sparkling, white gems. They weren't diamonds, but close enough. Or could she wear her blue denim dress? She loved that dress...and so did Eric. The white dress would do.

"That's a nice dress!" Beth stopped by her door.

Julie smiled. "I bought it after I saved up from working. Eric said it looked too nice on me."

Beth giggled. "And you chose it in spite of what he thought."

"This is the new me."

"Good for you. Enjoy the date. Nate is taking me roller skating. Have you done that?"

"No."

"We'll have to go sometime" She walked by.

Warmth filled Julie's body. Beth finally approved of her dating Andrew. She could relax. Before, Beth had wanted Julie to make sure she had peace and prayed about it. Did Beth notice how perfect they were for each other?

Julie wiped her sweaty palms on her sleeve.

As the doorbell rang, Julie had goosebumps. She straightened her dress, making sure it had no wrinkles. She had braided her hair instead of having it cascade down her shoulders.

Beth opened the door, and Andrew held flowers, his with mouth wide open. He wore a pair of black slacks and a white dress shirt. "Wow! You look amazing!"

"And so do you!" Her hands tingled as she took the flowers. He had put them in a vase.

"You two enjoy yourself!" Beth beamed.

"We will." He led her out to his BMW then he opened the door for her.

"Thank you." She slid in and buckled her seatbelt.

As he drove, he turned on his CD player. Hillsong "Whose I Am" played.

"So how was your week?"

"No job yet."

"It will come."

"I had a vision today. Someone from Montana is stalking me. I'm clueless as to who."

###

Heat boiled in his belly. She should know who! It was the same man who stalked her last week. He suspected the woman who threw the rock knew the man too. He would love to challenge him to a battle of wits. He might not be a match for him physically, but he was perfectly good at anything else. And why did he concern himself with that worthless scum? "Don't worry, Julie. If he comes face to face with you, I'll fight him." He scowled.

"Have they found the woman who threw the rock?"

He glared. "No."

Julie sulked. "I wish they would. Beth said the Corvette had a Montana license plate."

"The woman is from Montana too."

Julie's eyes grew big. "She knows that man!"

"Looks like trouble followed you." Her face reddened, and he patted her leg. "Don't worry. You are staying with Beth, so you're safe."

Julie smiled then glanced out the window.

"Any more word about you know who?"

"No. I told Mom that I was happy. I have told my mom of my intentions of not returning."

"He may end up back in jail anyway."

"I know. My mom has hopes. I have doubts."

He nodded. Just as well. Julie was his.

"This is a good song. I like it." She smiled.

"All their CDs are good. I have them all. Do you have any favorites?"

"Julie True. Beth introduced me to her. I also like Passion and Chris Tomlin."

He tingled with delight. "I like Chris too! We got something in common!"

The change of subject was a welcome change from the tension he had bottled up, but he wished he could have been there to protect her. Julie had become his concern since she told him about herself a couple of Sundays ago.

"Where are we going? I hope I'm not overdressed."

"To Eloise then dancing. You know how to dance?"

"You're looking at a country girl trying to fit into a city life."

He chuckled. "Square and line dancing?"

She nodded.

###

Outside Beth's apartment, Drew's neck and jaw stiffened. Julie's new friends were no match for him. Did Julie think she could evade him forever? One of these days he would catch them both off guard and not even his half-brother could rescue her. He looked forward to telling Eric that Julie was his. It would give him sheer happiness. He also sent the photo to Eric by snail mail. He didn't have his cell phone number.

Next to him was the lovely Lydia Cornell, a prostitute he had met at the bar the day he challenged Eric to a fight. However, Eric wimped out and wasn't even worthy of Julie.

"So, what's your plan, Drew?"

"Find a way to get into their apartment and hide. I need a distraction. So you'll call her friend and tell her you need her help."

Doubt was in Lydia's eyes. "And how would I do that? The police are after me!"

"Christians are good-natured people." He winked. "Just don't tell them your name."

###

Andrew's muscles tightened. Julie was unusually quiet, and she hardly touched her food. He drew his eyebrows together. "You okay?" He touched her hand.

"Trying to stay in God's presence."

Warmth flooded his body. As long as she stayed in His presence that bozo couldn't harm her. The man was no match for God. When he prayed that morning, he gave his anger and discontentment to God. He even surrendered Julie to Him, and peace had flooded his heart. He would help her grow in her faith. "That's good that you are doing that. God is here, and He is stronger than your enemies."

Her eyes widened in surprise. "Oh wow! That is the best thing you have ever said!" She smiled widely.

On the way to the dance hall, Julie's calm demeanor took his breath away. How could she be so relaxed after what she had been through? Had she truly given it to God? Her breaths came as easily as they went. He had no words for the woman beside him. Claudette was nothing like Julie, and his head spun. "Wow." He covered his mouth.

"Hmm?"

"You are amazing! Earlier you were uneasy, but you are relaxed now."

She giggled, but her eyes glowed.

"I was in his presence! It was wonderful!"

His heart soared. He wanted to marry her! Had he found his woman? Claudette had never sensed God's presence. Where had Julie been all his life? His eyes widened. He wanted this night to last forever.

###

As she basked in His love, all her stress and tension dissipated as if she had buried it in the jar and emptied into the bottomless pit. They belonged there. Worry, fear, and doubt belonged in hell. She would not allow the enemy to steal her peace and joy, especially not on her date with wonderful Andrew, who was all smiles. She delighted in his chuckles and silliness. Eric took life too seriously. "Thank you for this night," she said in a soft voice.

His eyes sparkled like glitter in the sand. "I have you to thank too. You helped me forget Claudette." He surprised her with a kiss, but not just any kiss. "I love you."

She moved close to him, her lips touching his. "I love you too."

Chapter 12

As Nate dropped Beth off, she caught an earful of whisperings. Was he here waiting for Julie? Her heart quickened its beat. *Someone is here.*

"Are you okay?" Nate startled her.

"I hear something, but I can't make it out."

Nate pulled out his gun, ready to defend Beth at any given time. "I'll follow you to your apartment."

Beth relaxed as Nate followed her to her apartment. She hated guns, but Nate wanted to protect her. She reached her bottom-floor apartment. She unlocked her door, with Nate behind her, still ready to fire.

As he stepped in, he checked every room, making sure her possessions were intact. "I don't see anything unusual."

"Nate, why would someone stalk Julie? What's the reason for that?"

He shrugged. "He wants revenge? Are you sure that Julie didn't know anyone driving a Corvette?"

"Yes. She said they all drive trucks. I would sure love to take a visit to Montana. Wouldn't you?"

His eyes glistened like the sun. "I would love to go anywhere with you...especially as your husband."

Her heart pounded. Was he going to propose? She had waited a year for this, but the timing wasn't right His eyes said he was, serious and she cleared her throat "What's going on?"

"Nothing. I love you." He kissed her lips, a silly grin on his face.

Huh? "We are in a middle of dangerous situation and you mention marriage?" Her eyebrows rose.

Nate narrowed his eyes, his gun posed. "I'll be back!" He ran out the door.

Beth took slow and cautious movements toward the window. Was there a Corvette out there? Nate headed toward the parking lot. Did he see something? He disappeared around the building. *Oh, God, keep us safe.*

Nothing made sense. Beth hadn't sensed danger until Julie arrived. It was as if she had brought it with her. Or could it be that the devil wanted to keep her in Montana, so he tried to frighten her to return. "DEVIL, IN JESUS'S NAME, FLEE!" Beth went to her room and played her collection of worship music and sang the songs that were on it as her weapons.

A few minutes later, Nate returned, his gun in its holster, and he glanced around. "It's gone." He pulled her close.

"I figured it out! The enemy of our souls wants Julie back in Montana."

"Why?"

"Because she's growing here, and he doesn't like it. Julie said her family is Baptist. She may go back with what she learned, but all the worries and cares she had back there would come back."

He touched her face. "Including Eric?"

"He's out on bail." Her smile faded.

"Then maybe it's him. He wants her back."

Beth shook her head. "No. I don't sense it. It's more evil than how she portrays Eric."

"Funny how I haven't sensed anything. Usually, I sense danger around you three sensed danger."

"I know."

"Let's pray."

She nodded.

Before they prayed, a car door slammed, followed by the front door opening. Julie eyes shone as she ambled into the apartment. "I sensed His presence tonight. It was so awesome!" She swooned.

Beth caught her breath. Julie sensed God's presence? She had to know more. Julie's experience had caused her to forget their discussion. "Do tell."

"Well, I'll leave you two. Call me if you need anything." Nate kissed her lips then ambled out, closing the door behind him.

"You sensed His presence?" Her voice softened as she slid in next to Julie.

"Oh, yes! I felt his peace, joy, and love!" Her eyes danced. "And Andrew says he hopes I never go back to Montana."

Beth nodded. "Have you felt like you were in danger in Montana?"

"No. Why?" Her eyes widened. "You think I should return?"

"No, but the devil wants you to. You are becoming that woman God wants you to be, and Satan hates it."

"I never thought of that."

"You could take all you have learned here, but you would go back to what you had and lose what you've gained." She raised her eyebrows.

"Hmm." Julie touched her lips. "As far as I am concerned, I'm staying. Andrew told me he loves me. I'm not going to give up."

"Good for you."

"Well, I'm exhausted. I'm going to bed."

"Me too."

Beth made sure all the windows and doors were locked.

###

The phone rang in middle of the night, waking Beth. Who could be calling her at midnight? Julie was in the next room. Beth calmed her mind as she answered the phone. "Hello?"

"Is this Beth Miller?" a brusque woman asked

"Yes."

"I need your help. Can you come to my place?"

Beth narrowed her eyes; her heart thumped. "Who is this?"

"I'm from church. I heard about you from a friend."

"Name, please," she demanded, her voice firm.

"Lauren."

"I don't know a Lauren. I think you have the wrong number."

"It's about the man who is stalking your friend. I saw him!"

Beth's ears picked up some background noises, but she couldn't discern them. "You saw who?"

"Please come! Your friend's life is in danger if you don't."

Beth's muscles tightened. "Listen whoever you are! We are protected by God's angels—"

Click

"Beth, who was that on the phone?"

"She said her name is Lauren. Do you know a Lauren?"

Julie sighed. "No."

"*She* says your life is in danger."

"Well, if it is, God is protecting me."

"That's right. He is. Good night."

Beth let the tension out. Julie had no concerns, so why should she? "Good night." She laid her head on the pillow.

###

Drew roared. "What happened?"

"She used her holy shit on me."

He raised his eyebrows. "And you let that offend you? You are as weak as Eric." He grabbed her hand as she was about to strike him. He glared. "I wouldn't try if I were you."

"I'm not weak! I just don't care to hear it!" Her eyes blazed. "Maybe you should look at yourself in the mirror."

His muscles quivered. He ought to slap that woman good. No woman should talk to him that way. Who was she to talk insolently to him and show him disrespect? "I have the power to expose you for who you are!" He raised his fist. "So consider your words."

Fury was in her eyes. "You can't do anything without me! I could easily tell the police that you stalked her. I could turn on you!"

His arm swung back, and he struck her hard in her face, causing it to bleed. He stormed out of his car and ran out. "I'll take care of Julie myself."

###

Eric's heart raced as he woke from a nightmare. In it, chains and shackles chained him to the wall while he watched in horror Drew making love to Julie.

"She is all mine. I have her under my spell...unless," he turned and sneered, "you agree to give me the ranch."

As Julie's eyes showed fear, he struggle to break free. The chains bound him tightly. "The ranch is not yours to take and neither is she!"

Drew laughed as his lips drew near Julie.

Eric moved his heavy body off the bed. How could he help Julie? Just as in his nightmare, he was helpless. He needed the power of God in his life. Without it, he was no match. *If I hadn't taken that phone call...* Eric bowed his head. *I'm starting to know you, but I don't know much. Keep Julie safe, please*

After his prayer, he drifted to sleep.

###

After Julie rolled all her cares unto the Lord, warmth tingled through her limbs. God had kept her safe from evil, and Beth and she had rest on either side. Sometimes Nate or Andrew would take turns spending the night on the couch, and they made them feel safe. It seemed the danger had passed.

Two days later, hope bubbled up in her heart when her phone rang. "Hello?"

"How bad do you want this job?" Beth asked.

"Huh?"

"Becaaaaauuuse," she drew out the word, "Marylin's assistant hired you."

She gasped. Did she hear right? She had to fall down, laughing.

"What's funny?"

"I was about to give up. When you told me about Vickie, I thought for sure she would hire me. Why now?"

"God's timing. Maybe He wanted you to trust Him instead of putting your hope in people. Anyway, come in and sign some paperwork."

"I'll be there in ten minutes."

As she drove to the book store, gratitude filled her heart. She had almost decided to try Sacramento because the city had more job opportunities than Marysville. She liked the small town feel.

She made friends who helped her grow in her faith. All four were nothing like her worldly friends in Montana. God had blessed her. "God, thank you for answering my prayers." He had filled her life with His goodness.

###

That afternoon, as customers trickled in and out of the store, all the tension Beth had carried oozed out of her body and disappeared into nothing. She felt warm all over. How could she ever repay God for answering her prayers?

The past week, Julie's life had been in danger, but God had protected her and given her peace. Now Julie could help pay rent, and they would continue their friendship.

She had lost all hope of having Julie as a roommate and co-worker, but that morning, God came through, and He overwhelmed her with His goodness. For that cause, she wanted to celebrate.

The door opened, creating quite a breeze as Julie stepped in. She had such a peaceful appearance on her face, and her face shone. "I'm here to sign papers."

"You've been with Jesus! I see it on your face!"

Julie nodded, beaming. "Today is a new day."

"Go back there. Vickie is waiting to meet you."

Julie walked around the counter and headed toward the back room. "Hi! I am Julie Henshaw!"

Vickie gasped. "Are you a native of Montana? When were you born?"

"Huh? Yes, and I was born over 24 years ago in Helena."

Vickie slapped her knee! "Yes! That's where I was born too! Are your parents Earl and Eleanor?"

Beth caught her breath. This conversation was getting interesting. No customers needed helped, so she inched away from the counter.

"Yes. Yes, it is!" Was Julie trying to place the name?

"I need to sit."

The bell on the counter rang. Beth tried not to lower her head. It was not her business anyway. Beth rang the items for the customer, her heart still full for what God had done.

Minutes later, Julie came out with tears in her eyes, but smiling. "I have a sister I didn't know about."

Beth's heart warmed. Now she could have two sisters in the same work place. How awesome was that? How awesome was

God who caused Marilyn to step down so Julie could meet Vickie and work at the bookstore? "That is great," she said with a light voice. "You've always wanted a sister."

Julie nodded, her smile slipping. Was she remembering her envying Andrew? "I feel bad. I have been so jealous, and yet God is so good to me. I should call Mom and ask her why she gave Vickie up."

"Please don't." Victoria came out of the backroom. "They may have a reason for giving me up."

"Victoria, how did you find out they were your parents?"

"I knew when my adoptive parents raised me, I was different. They were good people and religious, which I appreciated, so I didn't ask until I was eighteen. My adoptive parents moved us to California when I was eight."

"Wow." Beth had no words. "So you're older."

"By two years." Julie beamed, and she hugged Victoria.

Beth tried not to stare, but it was hard. How was it that Julie could have a boyfriend in such a short time, a job in less than a month, *and* find a sister she never knew she had, and yet life didn't come easy for Beth? She never had a sister. She faked her happiness. "That's great." Beth stalked away from them.

###

After work, the Lord laid it on Julie's heart to talk to Beth. Beth's attitude had puzzled her. Why did Beth act jealous? Did she envy her new-found sister? Shouldn't she be happy for her friend? "Beth, can I talk to you?"

Chapter 13

Julie's eyes showed hurt, and Beth hid her mouth behind her hand. "Sure. She looked away.

"Are you jealous?"

Beth pushed down the lump that formed in her throat. She resented Julie for asking her that. They were friends. How could she ask her such a question? "Whaaaaat? Nooo waay!" She shook her head vigorously.

"Because you were giving me that vibe. I saw your face turn red too."

Shame filled her. "Well." She stared at the floor. "I never had a sister."

"Neither did I, but I had good godly parents who raised me according to the Bible. They loved me, and I would have hope your parents loved on you."

"They did." Her voice softened. "Forgive me?"

"Of course." She gave Beth a hug.

With Julie forgiving her, she had a great day to make up for the way she acted. "Let's invite the guys for dinner and celebrate your new job."

"Sounds like a plan."

###

That evening as Julie went through her clothes, her ears picked up feet shuffling. It didn't come from Beth's room. Outside a cat meowed, causing her heart to race. She had to calm down. Julie moved close to the door.

"Julie?" Beth called, but she jumped. Her eyes grew big. "We're safe. It might be my neighbors. I'll go check." She walked toward the door.

She slowed her heart as movement outside her window caught her attention. "Anyone out there?" Her eyes narrowed in confusion.

"Look who I brought in!" Beth's voice gave Julie gave her a scare. "Wow! You're intense. The guys said they didn't see anyone snooping around." Beth came in with Nate and Andrew

Julie calmed her heart, trying to catch her breath. "He may have run—you have a gun?" she asked Andrew.

"For safety and protection." His lips pursed. "I love you, and I want to protect you."

Her heart warmed. "Thank you."

Andrew made her feel safe as he came near. She lost herself in his eyes of green. "Nate and I decided that you go with me, and she goes with him. We want our women close."

Julie nodded in agreement. She'd had enough excitement in one day. She couldn't wait to share her news.

In his car, she strapped herself in as a sense of calm came over. He always made her feel safe, but God's protection was best.

"Since we got the license plate number, we found the car was a rental from Montana. Bozeman's Car Rental leased it to Drew McDermott." He gazed at her. "Ring a bell?"

She shook her head. "Should it?"

He began driving, still not smiling. "I think he tracked you down, waited until he could follow you. You said Eric was in jail when you left?"

She nodded.

"With him in jail, this guy could hunt you down without Eric coming to your aid."

She heated up. Eric's not in jail—wait, that was a month ago? Who did Eric know? Nothing made sense. Julie grimaced. "I don't get it."

Andrew frowned. "Let's try to enjoy ourselves."

Julie tried to relax. "Okay."

"I remember how relaxed and safe God made you feel? Stay in it."

She nodded.

###

Julie didn't have much of an appetite. They hadn't found Drew or that woman who threw the rock. She had to keep staying in God's presence. Since when did life become a warfare? Nothing happened much in Montana. She worked and went home. Why had she moved to California? To attract unwanted people?

Her fingers itched to call Eric...that was, if he was not in jail. Maybe he knew who Drew and Lydia were. But she had no desire to return to Montana. She only wished she could enjoy life without having to look over her shoulder.

Andrew looked worried. "Penny for your thoughts?"

"Why haven't they found those two?" She wrinkled her brow.

Andrew shrugged. "Beats me, but I'm here. I have my gun. Are you feeling His presence?"

"I'm trying."

"Are you anxious? Worried?"

She nodded.

"Be anxious for nothing. That's what Paul wrote."

Julie took a deep breathing, letting out the tension she felt as she placed it in God's hands. "Thank you."

His phone rang, and he checked it. "Nate." He put his phone to his ear. "Hello. What? They did? Well, hopefully she will!" The expression on his face lightened Julie's chest. "This is great news! Where did they find her? Yes! I will let her know. See you later." His smile stretched from cheek to cheek making Julie's skin tingle. "They found Lydia walking down the highway. They arrested her."

The news took her breath away, and she covered her mouth. The news excited her so much she couldn't think. Tears streamed down her face. "She could...would she..?"

"We can only hope she will rat on her partner."

"Hopefully, she was his only partner, and they will catch him soon."

He lifted up his glass of wine. "Let's toast to the news."

Joy filled her heart. God would take care of Drew with Lydia out of the way. Now she could focus on her relationship with Andrew. She wanted him in her life and without having people stalking her. She lifted her glass and clinked his. "Cheers."

She could only hope they would catch Drew.

###

Ever since Lydia walked out on him, Drew's muscles had tensed up. There was no one he could trust. He would go alone. He could do it! He didn't need a partner. He could easily destroy Eric single handedly. Eric loved Julie, did he? Would Eric love her if he raped Julie? Would he want her after Drew ravaged her?

For now, Drew would hide in darkness. He would make Julie think he had gone home. He had done well for himself. Her boyfriend never got his name, and he was quick like a bunny. He could go home and try to get some sleep. He needed to keep in darkness just in case Lydia ratted on him. Perhaps he could disguise himself.

Lydia had only gone along for the ride. He wouldn't put it past her to rat on him. He needed a loyal friend, but who?

A siren sounded in the distance, and his heart raced. He revved up his engine and drove off into the night. But he would not be satisfied until he could completely destroy Eric.

Chapter 14

A year later.

As Julie worshipped God, she fell into a trance. The hair on the back of her neck lifted as she had a vision of a man with a man getting off a train. "Who is he?"

"This man wants nothing more than to have you for himself."

"Is this the same man who stalked me?"

"Yes. And he is back for vengeance."

"Why? What have I done? Wasn't he arrested?"

"Eric still loves you, and this man will do anything to destroy him."

Julie lost her breath. "But he is serving a two-year jail time!"

"That doesn't matter to him. You must be on guard and continue to abide in me."

As the vision ended, God gave her the strength to pray. He had protected her before. He would do it again. She was not about to leave Marysville. It had become her home. She had dated Andrew for a year now, and she was ready for a proposal. She had a job she left. It wouldn't be fair if she left Marysville like she left Montana. God would have her back.

Julie closed her eyes and uttered words no human could understand....

Her cell phone chimed a worship song she loved, "Our God is Greater." A reminder that He was greater than her fears. "Hello?"

"Hi. It's Andrew."

Her heart danced. He had called at the right time. "Hi."

"I was praying and saw a man coming to your door. Are you okay?"

"I think so. I just need to spend time in prayer."

"Good to hear. Is it okay I come over...just in case?"

"You're so sweet. I love you," she said in her silly love-struck tone.

"Listen, I would feel safe knowing I could protect you. You're my girlfriend."

Julie's heart warmed. She loved his admission. She wanted him close to her too. "Come on over then."

"I'll be there shortly. Don't let anyone in. If you hear me say it's me, you can open the door."

"Okay."

"I love you too"

She hit end call. God had been good to her, sending Andrew her way. He filled her heart with thanksgiving.

The room chilled. Was he here now? She went to lock the door and closed windows. She dressed herself in God's armor and prayed in the spirit. She had no time for fear...

A half hour later, someone knocked at her door. "It's me Andrew!" The sound of his voice released the tension she kept bottled up. She let him in. "I called my sister. You are more than welcome to stay with her."

"Go with him."

"Okay. Let me pack quickly."

He glanced around. "Where's Beth?"

"At church. I fell asleep and woke up after she left. Where were you?"

"I didn't go. I had things on my mind."

While she packed, he looked out the window then ran out the door. Did he sense the stalker here now? He had his gun poised. "Oh sorry!" She heard him say. Who was he saying sorry to?

He returned to the apartment and fixed his green eyes on her. They mesmerized her. Love was in his eyes and a smile on his lips.

"Ready?" he asked.

"Not yet," she responded, and he pulled her in, and their lips met in a passionate embrace. She pulled away. "Mmm. That's not fair." Julie cracked a smile.

"I enjoyed it though." He touched her face.

"Me too."

After he helped her pack, he carried her two suitcases while she carried her garment bags to her red Ford Fusion. He held her in his arms before she climbed in. "I'll see you at my sister's."

She waggled her eyebrows as she smiled.

He released her and skipped to his car.

Great joy filled her heart. She didn't have to leave Marysville. Someday she would, when God called her to. God had answered her plea by sending Andrew her way. Whoever this threat was, Andrew would keep her safe, or she could move back home.

Who was Drew? Whenever God showed her his face, it was blurred, and He had revealed nothing, except her connection to Eric and his love for her. If only Eric would stop loving her.

###

Andrew stopped in front of a white, small one story house with a built-in garage. The front door opened and a petite young lady with long hair tied in an unusual braid ran out to Andrew as he climbed out of his car.

"Hi," Julie said, reaching to shake her hand. She had met Kelly before, and Andrew only teased her about Kelly. She was much of a free spirit.

"Hi, Julie. Nice to see you again. Andrew, get her bags. Come on inside." She led her in.

The interior the house left Julie breathless. Although the house was small in size on the outside, her living room had plenty of space. Stepping on the carpet was like stepping on clouds. She had one of those sliding glass doors Julie had always liked.

"I'll show you the room."

###

As Andrew followed, heat radiated in his chest. Julie would be safe at his sister's house. He wanted her to accept Julie as part of his life. When he first told Kelly about her, a look of concern was on her face.

"Make sure you don't break her heart and get arrogant on her." Kelly acted like an older caring sister, but she was more Julie's age.

"I won't. I promise."

And he hadn't. Each day God had shown him how to release his anger and pride to Him. Julie was an angel sent from God.

"She does seem like a nice person." She raised her eyebrows. "From Montana?"

"That's what she said." He smiled.

The women brought him out of his introspection when Kelly asked Julie a question. "Do you love him?"

Julie smiled to him with such warmth on her face. "Yes. I want to marry him."

His heart palpitated. "Well, I should get your garment bag, then I'm off."

Julie's mouth fell open. "You're not going to stay?"

"No, I better go. I will let you two talk girl talk."

As he headed out to his car, the hair on his arm stood on end. He kept a watchful eye on the road as he opened the passenger door. "He couldn't possibly follow us here." He took out the garment bag. "Though I walk through the valley of shadow of death..."

He made it back into her house "Okay. Here you go."

"Andrew, you okay? You look white?" Kelly asked.

"If you don't mind, I changed my mind. I'll sleep on the couch."

Both women exchanged glances.

###

When Kelly retired for the night, Julie's stomach turned to butter. Earlier, Andrew had turned pale. It was not good.

"You sensed danger?" She joined him on the couch.

He nodded. "Drew was an outlaw in Montana. That's what worries me."

"I knew nothing about the men in Eric's life, except his ranch hands."

"He's one big mystery." He gave her a concerned look.

She leaned into his arms. "I'm glad you are here."

"We have church in the morning. Allow me to take you?"

"You would have to go home and change."

"I don't live far from here." He had love in his eyes, and it warmed her heart.

"I would like it if you would."

He planted a kiss on her face and let her lean in his arms until they both fell asleep.

Darkness covered the forest, and branches broke under her feet. Her heart nearly dropped out of her chest as a man gave a command to her horse

The horse galloped closer and closer. The farther she ran, the louder the man's voice. "Giddyup!"

"Help me, Jesus!"

He who walks through the valley of the shadow of death...

Psalms 23! She used to recite it as a child! As she allowed the words to sink in deep, the man's voice grew fainter and fainter.

A bright light shone, dispelling darkness. She had lost her breath, and her smile widened

Julie opened her eyes. Calm and ease came over her. The nightmare turned dream gave her a sense of peace.

Andrew's snore caught her off guard. She had forgotten that she fell asleep in his arms.

"Good morning!" Kelly's greeting woke Andrew, and she giggled. "I hope you didn't... you know." She smiled.

"I had no idea I fell asleep here," Julie replied.

Andrew had a grin on his face. "I did. You felt good in my arms. I should go and get changed."

"Be back for breakfast?" Kelly asked,

"You bet" He ran out the door, leaving the women giggling.

"He loves you. The silly grin is because of you."

Before Julie could reply, her cell phone chimed. *Beth.* "Hi!"

"I got your note. Are you okay?" Beth sounded relieved.

"Yes. Andrew and Kelly have been good to me. Even Andrew sensed danger."

"Our apartment is cheap for one reason. I think it's time to get a house."

Her heart squealed. She had always wanted a house. Now that she worked full time and tithed regularly, God had blessed her. She couldn't wait to move. This would be great. "Yes, let's do!"

"And we will have a security system too."

Where they lived now, they didn't have one—the reason for the cheap rent. Why couldn't Beth afford a house before she came to Marysville? "I'm surprised you don't live in one now."

"I thought about it, but I'd rather share rent than pay a mortgage."

That made sense.

"Well, see you in church."

"See you also."

Beth ended the call.

Chapter 15

The silence between them weighed heavy on Julie's heart. He smiled, but his eyes were on the road. When he came back, he said little to her. "Penny for your thoughts?"

"I don't want to worry you."

"Are you afraid of losing me?" Why had she said that? She shook her head. "Never mind."

"How do you feel about California?"

"I love it here! Beth and I are going to get a house."

"Julie, will you do me a favor? Will you tell your parents about me?" His eyes showed love and concern. It warmed her heart. He reached to touch her face. "Or have you?"

Her stomach tensed. She didn't feel her parents would be happy for her. They still loved Eric even though he was in jail. Telling them would break their hearts. How could she answer him? "I thought you understood."

"We've dated for over a year."

"So why haven't you proposed?" she joked.

He winked, and her heart raced. "Why not answer my question first?" His smile helped her to relax. "I told my parents."

"I will. I promise."

"After last night, I got to thinking that I need to be a man for you. I love you so much. The minute I came to your rescue, I knew you were for me, but I was afraid to let you in."

"I felt the same way. I was all for myself. I realized that if I put myself…" She tried to ignore the lump in her throat. She needed to do it now. She took out her phone as she held her breath.

"Hello?" her father answered.

Andrew squeezed her hand, which comforted her. "This is Julie."

"Baby girl, how are you? Mom is worried sick about you."

She gave Andrew a nervous smile. "I'm wonderful. Moving to California has happened to me...and I ...I have someone in my life," she said as Andrew's eyes shone.

There was silence then: "You do?"

Andrew's reassuring smile gave her the courage to go on. "I'm not moving back home."

More silence.

"Dad?"

"Julie, honey. It's Mom. Your dad...has fainted."

Julie tensed up, and she tried to cool down. She had tried to tell Andrew. Why couldn't he understand? *I tried to see it from his point of view. I did it to put his mind at ease.* She wanted to ball up her fist, but she took in some slow steady breaths. "Why is it that I find someone I love, and you're not happy for me? You never have been!" She shut off her phone. "I knew this would happen."

"But you told them, so trust God with the rest." He wiped her tears while keeping his eyes on the road. "I'm proud of you."

But Julie wouldn't look at him.

###

A lump formed in Andrew's throat and nausea hit him. He wished he had more understanding. Although he had a strict father, his parents loved on them. *I should have listened to her instead of insisting.* Did he blow it? Over the year, God had softened his heart, so he had no defense. He closed his eyes. *God help me to see where she is coming from.*

"Julie has fears. Have faith. She will release them."

Julie stared out the window, but a tear had fallen. Was she afraid of losing him? What was she afraid of? She had told him that her parents wanted her to marry Eric—she was afraid of letting her parents down!

"Oh, Julie! My love."

Another tear fell.

Relief refreshed him like an oasis in the desert as he arrived. God could speak to Julie's heart about her fears, and Andrew would pray for her. As he led her inside, her sadness turned to happiness as if she had never had that phone call.

As the pastor preached on fears, Julie gasped then the tears came. His heart warmed. God had spoken to her. Joy filled his heart as her lips parted

"She needs to feel safe with me."

Andrew nodded. God was right. Although he could be there for her, he could not protect her without God. He needed to show Julie that His love—God's love—could cast out her fears. Many years ago, he learned that himself. When he was six years old, someone locked him in the closet. It was an accident, but he could never forget how it affected him. He hoped that the devil wouldn't lock Julie into any fear.

After church, they took a walk. She had a lot on her mind, but he waited. "What did you think of the message?" he asked, trying to gauge her response.

"I thought I didn't have any fears, but I did. When I witnessed Eric carrying a rolled-up carpet, I feared the worst. I allowed the devil to gain a foothold in my life." She wiped the tears from her eyes. "I suppose if I was rational, I would still be there. I don't regret coming here." She smiled to him. "I might take a trip to Montana, but I'm not sure when."

"And your parents?"

"I knew I would let them down, which was why I didn't tell them. I wasn't angry with you. I was angry at God."

She had taken a load off his mind with her confession. She's angry—her parents—not him? His muscles weakened. Gratitude filled his heart. "I thought I had upset you."

"When I was talking to you, it came to me that you were right. I love you, and here I am wanting to keep you as a secret. My big fear, if you want to know, is Eric coming back into my life."

"He's in jail."

"But not for long. I found out from my friend Jordan that he is doing time for two years for aiding and abetting."

"Eric didn't kill anyone?"

She nodded. She stopped and gazed into his eyes. He watched her struggle to find words. "I need to take a trip home. I would love for you to go with me, but—"

"I would love to go with you!" He held her his arms, her warm skin next to his. Her heart beating with his.

"Then let's plan a day where we could go together...in separate cars. They need to meet you."

"I agree." He put his arm around her. "Ready to head back."

"I guess."

"You guess?" He raised his eyebrows. "Are you sure of anything?"

Her eyes sparkled. "Of my love for you." She touched his face, but he brought her close, his lips to hers. She pulled away. "I think we should wait until after marriage."

His heart fluttered, and he waggled his eyebrows. "Oh yeah?"

Her mouth dropped open, and she ran. "You have to catch me first!"

He chased her and caught her in his arms. She had the prettiest blue eyes that glistened as the reflection on the water. "I caught you. Now what will you do?"

Julie grinned as he put her arms around his shoulders. "That's no fair. You have the upper advantage."

He chuckled. "I guess I do." He released her. "You bring out the beast in me."

On the way home, the mood lightened since they had a little fun. Julie looked amazing even after running out of breath. Her beauty just took his breath away. "I would like to see you again."

She smiled, her face turned up. "I would love to see you too. I work from 9 to 5. I have to see when Beth wants to go to house hunting."

"Call me or text me. Okay?"

She kissed his cheeks. "I will."

###

Julie had the house to herself as Kelly was not home. A note on the table got her attention.

Hey, Julie.

Not trying to get rid of you, but look this up on the web. www.KLhomes.com. They price their homes as low as $55,000. I think with the jobs you and your friend have you can afford it. I'm out with my fiancé, so I won't be home until tonight. Help yourself to what's in the kitchen.

–Kelly

Warmth filled Julie's heart. She wanted to make it up to Kelly for her hospitality. What could she do to show her appreciation? She didn't write what time she would be back. So making dinner may be a good idea. She had an immaculate house. Of course! Although she worked full time, couldn't she help with the housework? In the meantime, she felt the need to spend time with Jesus.

As she listened to inspirational music, she allowed the words to speak to her. She immersed herself in God's love. Her limbs tingled. Tears fell. *Oh, Jesus! I love Andrew so much! Earlier, I sensed he was going to propose to me. Now I have a feeling, I won't see him again. Am I being irrational?* Two years ago, she anticipated the same thing from Eric, but the phone call happened. She didn't want her heart to break again.

Julie stilled her heart and closed her eyes. "Lord, I give you my anxious thoughts."

As she waited, she saw a vision of a man on a horse and a lasso in his hand. Was this Eric? Was he not in jail? "God, who is he?"

"He is a man after your own heart."

Her skin tingled. "There are two after me now?"

"Yes, but one is not dangerous as you might think".

Eric? Was he talking about Eric? Not now! She had moved on and found someone to love. Could she say goodbye to Andrew? Beth's words haunted her. *You owe it to him to tell him the truth*

"This can't be happening to me!" She threw a pillow across the room.

"Julie, be still. Know that I am God."

"I'm sorry, God. I'm...just not ready to face him."

"This is not immediate future, and I will prepare you".

Earlier, she wanted Andrew to go with her. Now she had her doubts. They should marry first before going there as a couple. What was she afraid of? That she would renew her love for Eric? She looked within her heart. If Eric was coming for her, she would have to let Andrew go and say goodbye to him. She wished that day would never come.

The doorbell rang. Her heart raced. Julie got up and walked to the door. She relaxed. It was Beth. She let her in. "Come in!"

Beth rushed in. "He came to the apartment!"

"Who?"

"Oh my goodness! He had such dark eyes!"

She gasped. "You saw Drew?"

"Just his eyes. Thank goodness. Nate answered the door. The guy said he was looking for his sister." Beth rolled her eyes.

"Yeah right." She closed the door and led Beth to the couch. "Why didn't you call the police?"

"Nate did, but when the police got there, the man had disappeared. He's elusive." Her mouth fell open. "You're listening to Julie True!" She smiled from ear to ear.

"Yes, it calms my heart."

Beth noticed her frown. "What happened? He broke up?"

Julie giggled. "No of course not. It's just that...I have a lot on my mind."

"Hmm. I see. I'm glad Kelly let you stay here."

"I hope he didn't follow you."

Her eyes widened. "I do too! Sorry if he did." She joined her on the couch. "I found a couple of houses near Marysville where we could look."

"Kelly says KL homes have good prices."

"Are you sure?"

"Let's look them up."

"What about Andrew? Why didn't she mentioned Andrew?"

"Let me call him and see what he thinks." She took out her phone, her heart pounding.

"Hey, Julie!"

Her stomach fluttered. "Hi. I have a question. How much are the homes you sell? Are they cheaper than KL?"

Beth gasped. "Julie!"

Andrew chuckled. "I would be glad to help you find a house. How did you find out about KL Homes?"

"Your sister."

"KL stands for Kathy Lane. She's Kelly's friend."

"Oh."

"And the lowest priced homes are sixty-five thousand. I can get you a house for less than that."

Hope bottled up in her chest. "You can?"

"Did you think I couldn't?" There was a tease in his voice.

"Okay. When can you show us?"

"Let me gather up the list of houses that are available...and we can meet for lunch tomorrow to discuss it. Bring Beth."

Beth's eyes were wide with very few blinks, and she smiled. Julie would have no problem bringing her. "I will. Where shall we meet?"

"Let's see. My lunch break is 12:15pm. Do you want to go to Denny's?"

"I like Denny's. Sure."

"I'll see you then,"

"Okay. I love you."

"I love you too." Was he grinning? She giggled then ended the call. "I have a question. Why didn't you move out before now?"

"My roommate preferred an apartment and, I couldn't afford a house with just one person. I told you that."

"Oh. Aren't you glad you have me?"

"More glad than ever."

Chapter 16

Two weeks later, Julie's insides vibrated. Andrew sold them a single story house. The house had a master bedroom, which Beth claimed, and a guest bedroom. It was the perfect size for them. The front room accommodated their spiritual needs. And it was only about a mile to work.

Julie and Beth bumped shoulders with each other and high fived. Julie gasped. The front room had a sliding glass door. She had always wanted one.

"Just sign the paper work and it is yours." Andrew smiled ear to ear.

"Thank you so much," Beth said.

The back door led to average-sized backyard. A tree on either side. She sat down and closed her eyes. At one time, she had lived in a small town and with her parents. She had a full heart. How could she repay God for giving her the desires of her heart? It wasn't marriage she wanted. What if she wouldn't be happy living on the ranch? *If Eric agrees to live here in California, I will let go of Andrew.* Why did she pray that? She loved Andrew! Or had God sent him for a season. *Not your will but my will.*

###

Andrew's body tensed up. Amidst their excitement, Julie had walked out and now sat under a tree. Her mood had changed. Was it Eric? Drew?

"Why don't you go out to her?" Beth suggested.

"Has she been like this?" He scratched his head.

"Not usually, but she has been having nightmares. She won't share them with me."

"I'll see what I can do."

"I'll be praying."

He joined Julie on the ground and leaned close to her. "Are you okay? You can tell me."

Julie glanced back then to the ground, not looking at him. "Nightmares." Her eyes were sad.

"About?" He lowered his voice.

"A cowboy on a horse."

"Drew?"

She shook her head. "He said I had to make a choice."

"He?" He raised his eyebrows. "Eric?"

Tears fell from her eyes as she leaned on Andrew.

"You...still love him."

"I know more about you than I do about him, but a part of me is drawn to that part of him."

"How did you meet Eric?"

"I was waiting tables. He came in for a meal, and I guess he stole my heart that day."

"Did you ever get it back?" He sensed Eric hadn't gotten her heart completely.

"If I tell Beth, she would lecture me about breaking your heart."

"Eric is in jail?"

A small smile appeared on her face.

"I think I understand you now. You feel if you leave California, you'll never come back."

She nodded. "I think Drew is connected to Eric."

"Like he hired him?"

"No, I don't think that's his nature."

A heaviness settled in his body. Should he let her go? After she announced she wanted to buy a house, he had to put his plans on hold. He couldn't ask her to marry him. Yet on the other hand, Julie felt safe with him. They could have a long engagement. Would that work? He fingered the ring in his pocket.

His heart beat strong. The woman he loved sat next to him. Her long red hair flowed down her back, smelling of lavender. He nuzzled his nose in her hair.

"Are you ever sorry you met me?"

"No." His lips parted, inviting her to kiss him.

She punched him! "Is that how you respond?"

"Julie, I don't care, okay? And don't worry about Beth. You take care of Julie. Let God deal with her."

"Even after I told you my nightmares?"

"Yes! Because I love you! Dang it, Julie!"

A playful smile appeared on her face then she lean on him.

###

Beth's muscles weakened. She thanked God that Andrew hadn' left or stormed back into the house. Andrew had stayed a long time with Julie. She worried that Julie would leave Andrew. Julie hadn't shared with her, but Andrew might share what Julie told him. She pressed her hand to her stomach. *Thank you, Jesus*

Andrew rose to his feet and walked in. "She asked me not to tell you. She is concerned you will lecture her." His eyes showed seriousness. "Beth, I'm thirty years old. I'm old enough to take care of myself." His lips pressed together. "She has told me in not so many words that she needs me, but she needs God more." He walked to the front door. "See you and Nate tonight at the movie." He smiled.

Beth's tension slowly dwindled away. "Yeah. See you."

He left.

"God, he is something else. I just hope we can both marry our men."

###

Before Andrew and Nate arrived, Julie's heartbeat throbbed in her throat. She hadn't sensed any danger in the past month, but she'd had nightmares. Her visions differed from her nightmares. As she sat still, her mind on God, her heart raced. She saw a dark shadow following Andrew.

"He has come to take your happiness. If your happiness is in me, then he can't take it."

And he will leave Andrew alone?

"Andrew is in my care."

The weight of her burdens lifted, and she let out a breath. *Thank you! Thank you!* "Happiness is to know thy savior, living a life within his favor..." Julie covered her mouth. Andrew was not her happiness, Jesus was.

The doorbell rang. "They're here!" Beth called.

After she freshened up, she went out, turning off the lights. Tonight, she would focus on the revelation and enjoying the movie with her friends.

Andrew smiled. "You look lovely. Are you ready?" He took her hand.

"Yes."

On the way, Julie spoke her heart. "Thank you for coming out like you did." She leaned on him.

"I care."

"I had a talk with Jesus. I realize I was putting my happiness in you. Did you sense any darkness?"

His mouth dropped open. "On the way here! Wow! Did God give you a vision?"

"Yes, Satan wants to take my happiness from me"

His lips parted. "I'm your happiness?"

"Was. I put my happiness in Jesus. You remember that song?"

"Happiness is to know the savor living a life with in his favor," he sang. "I love that song!"

Heat radiated in her chest "Beth taught me a lot. She said always seek God first. We have such great fellowship, but I think I need to do something for others."

"That's a great idea!" he said energetically.

"I'll see where I can volunteer at church."

He smiled.

Chapter 17

A month later

Andrew and Nate helped the ladies move into their house. Nate followed Andrew in. "Are you going to tell her sometime?"

"I don't want to ruin her spirits."

Julie narrowed her eyes. "Tell me what?"

Andrew glanced at his brother as if he wished Nate would keep quiet.

Beth came out, looking at the men. "What's going on?"

"We're moving," Nate said it.

"You and Andrew?" Beth asked; even she didn't know.

"Our father is sick. Julie, his cancer has gotten worse. I wish you could go with us."

As Julie was about to respond in anger, God filled her with His peace and calmed her heart. Andrew still loved her. She could still date him. This was a time to draw close to God. "I wish I could too, but I'll be okay"

His eyes glowed. "You have changed a lot. I will text you, but one more thing." He took out of his pocket a small box

She lost her breath as he showed her a 12 karat diamond ring. "Now? You are going to propose now?"

"I have waited too long. I had fears also. I was afraid of losing you, but I realized that God put you in my life for a reason. I'll give you time to think about it." He touched her face. "We will only be a few hours away." He put the ring in his pocket, as she hadn't given him her answer.

"Where do your parents live?"

"They live near San Francisco. We moved here to get away from the wickedness."

His touch gave her a jolt. "How long will you be there?"

"I don't know. My father had stage 2 cancer, but now it is worse."

"Doesn't he believe that God heals?"

"He does, and he is fighting the best he can, but chemo is weakening him."

"Call me or text me?" She lost herself in his green eyes.

"Every day if I can. But remember our song? When you are sad?"

She nodded. "In the savior."

"And living in his favor." His lips parted, and she moved in close to kiss him. "I love you."

"Same here." He kissed her.

###

The following day, as Andrew stacked his clothes in his suitcase, her body heat rose. He packed the same way her father packed, and his mannerism was the same as Eric's. "You pack like my daddy!"

He smiled as he packed in his shaver. "I'll take that as a compliment." He straightened up and looked lovingly at her. "I still would like to meet your parents."

He stomach quivered. How could he meet her parents if they were far from each other? She agreed to it before he announce they were moving. San Francisco was farther away from Bozeman than Marysville. "I hope you can."

"Don't hope, know. Have faith. If God is for us…"

"Who can be against us?"

"Keep the faith." He kissed her lips.

She nodded. "I will." She returned the kiss, but held onto him.

Andrew lost track of time and ran out to his car. He threw the suitcase in the back.

"What's the hurry? You're not taking a plane or train," she asked from the doorway.

He gave her a silly grin. "No, but if I stay longer, I might never go." He blew her a kiss and hopped into his car.

###

Something happened as he drove off. Her breath came a little easier. Andrew's move was not the end, but the beginning of a new life. God brought him into her life to help her grow. The same with Beth. A year ago, she was a selfish, twenty-four-year-old woman, full of fear and worry. Was it time to face Eric? Could she love him again, knowing that he had been in jail? Would she love him anyways? Or could she say goodbye? Could she?

Beth embraced her. "Julie, I have been wanting to tell you. I heard this voicemail. The call was from yesterday when you were outside."

Julie couldn't breathe. Had Beth snooped on her phone calls? How many others had she heard? She felt her anger rise, but who was it for? Beth had always been there for her. She had supported her. Beth had her reasons. Julie gritted her teeth. "O...kay."

"You have ten new voicemails," the voice said as Beth frowned.

"My parents mostly."

"They may be overprotective, but they love you." She skipped to the last voicemail. "Brace yourself."

She did.

"Julie, I love you. I am so sorry for taking that call. I'm sorry I pushed you away. I know you did it, but I'm not hurt or angry. You did it to save me...Julie I hope I can see you again..."

The words she longed to hear were like music to her ears and healing for her soul. Eric, in all of his life, had never touched her heart like that. The tears came freely, but they were tears of joy. "Just as I let go of Andrew, you play it." She smiled through her tears. "You have been my very best friend." She sat on the couch. "I didn't realize until now that I have denied my heart's desire. I had two really, but I couldn't have one without the other."

"Did you sense it in his voice?" She softened her tone.

Julie nodded. "He said," more tears came, "I did it to save him, but it was God." Julie sobbed, and Beth held her in her arms. "I have to say goodbye to Andrew, and I can't."

"I think he sensed it too. We had a talk. I asked him. 'Are you prepared if Eric comes back into her life?' He didn't like hearing it, but he said, yes."

"What...? But I thought… He proposed."

Her eyes sparkled.

Julie gasped. "That was a test?"

"You didn't say yes right away. He knew."

"Oh my goodness! He left with such grace."

"You gave him the best year of his life! Before you came, he was all about work. He thought if he poured himself into his job, he would forget about Claudette. Claudette couldn't handle his cockiness, but you did."

Julie had no words.

Chapter 18

A week later

Sunday night Eric arrived in Marysville, and his heart enlarged. God had led him here with the help of Earl and Eleanor. The two had been like parents to him ever since Julie became his girlfriend. They stood by his side while he served time for a crime he hadn't committed. Just as Joseph served time for a crime he didn't commit—they had to forgive. His mission? To find the woman who stole his heart and win hers. Did she get his voicemail?

And yet, as he drove through the small town of Marysville, his skin prickled. He suspected Drew was here. Drew had better hope he didn't reveal himself to her, or she would know without a doubt. The sole reason he wanted her to move in was to protect her. Now, God was her protector. He was not worried.

As he turned down Oak Drive, his heart fluttered. Julie was close by. On this street. Was hers fluttering too? Fluttering like a bird in a tree?

His heart pumped, and his pulse raced. A black Corvette sped past him. Eric stepped on the gas and followed the Corvette. His gut told him that Drew was in that car. Drew was on a high speed race. His truck was not equipped for high speed races. *Lord, is he going to her house?* Why was he speeding?

"He's leading you on a chase."

How did he know…? My license plate.

"Yes."

Eric turned left and remained at the speed limit. He would leave Drew in God's hands.

Fifteen minutes later, he arrived at a small one story house. A conviction in his heart that she lived here. He hopped out of his truck and knocked on the door.

His feet froze. A redheaded woman stood at the door. Was this Julie? His mind went blank. He couldn't think. He couldn't move a muscle. His vision blurred as spots danced before his eyes. "Is that you, Julie?"

She giggled as she helped him come inside. "I know, I dyed my hair, but the Lord helped you find me," her muffled voice said. "I was...uh... expecting you." She closed the door. "My housemate is in San Francisco." She helped him sit on the couch as she sat.

"You...know he helped me?" Did he hear right?

"Yes. So when did it happened and how?"

"You dyed your hair?"

Julie had an amusing smile on her face. "Do you like it?"

He rubbed his eyes.

When shock had worn off, he took in the surroundings. The house had Julie's name all over it. She may have dyed her hair, but posters of country life adorned the walls, including posters of scriptures on them. "Trust the Lord with all your heart and lean not on your understanding." He smiled and nodded. "I missed you so much."

A tear fell down her face. "I thought I was over you. I told you on the phone, but you didn't believe me."

"I came because I had to know, to find out if you really were."

"I met a man. He reminds me of you. He could be a city version of you for all I know. When he moved, I didn't fall apart as I thought I would. Beth played the voicemail, and that was when I realized that I still loved you." Another tear fell.

"I'm a changed man, Julie. Your parents will tell you that. They missed you."

Julie wiped her tears. "Could you forgive me?"

"You know what Joseph said? He said what you meant for my evil, God had turned it for my good. I found God in prison. His grace saved me!"

###

As Eric sat in that recliner, telling her how God saved him, tears of joy flooded her eyes. Eric was here. God had answered her prayers. And as he spoke, love and forgiveness was in his eyes. She stood and made slow movements toward him. He stood and held his arms out. She fell into his embrace. "God blessed the broken road that led you to me."

Her heart danced as he held her close. The smell of Old Spice delighted her senses. He smelled of home. His closeness brought joy to her soul. Had she really missed him this much? He made her heart sing. They were two birds of a feather. She pulled away and gaze into his brown eyes. "Tell me about your prison life."

"Do you really want to know? I want to hear about you. You have a housemate? Are you happy here? Do you want to live here instead of Montana?" he said it too quickly.

"Wait slow down!" She giggled, looking up at him. "The night is still young. How about a ride in your truck, and I can answer all your questions." She covered her mouth. "I'm sorry. You are probably tired. I just got excited"

A silly grin on his face. "It's okay, babe. Finding you gave me the extra energy needed. Shall we?"

Julie's heart pounded. They had a lot to catch up on. Over a year of not seeing each other. She wanted to hear how God had gotten him a shorter sentence. She couldn't wait to catch up.

"Are you hungry? I noticed Denny's is open."

"How about a drive through?"

"Even better!" She followed him out the door.

###

While driving, Eric's heart skipped a beat. His Julie was with him, and he had one request. Will she say yes? "The night of our last date, I should have proposed to you, but I couldn't handle marriage, yet I wanted to protect you. I realize God was your protection."

She nodded. "Although, you kept me from having a close relationship with him."

"I'm sorry." He touch her face and held her hand for a while. "We can have it together, go to church together. But wouldn't it be wonderful if we could read the Bible together...in our bedroom?"

Her mouth fell open, and her eyes grew big. "Are you..." She covered her mouth.

He chuckled. "Why do you think I asked you where you want to live?"

Julie stared out the window. "Are you willing…" She shook her head. "What did you do with my Eric?"

He pulled over so he wouldn't get into accident. His heart pounded as he gazed at her. "Your eyes are like the color of sapphires."

She blushed, but a tear fell. "I think I'm dreaming." He answered her with a pinch. "Ow!"

He chuckled. "You're not dreaming. This is as real as my love for you."

"When we met, you charmed my heart away, and when I told my parents, they approved. But I didn't really know you. I still don't, so let's do this. Let's date again, and when you are ready you can share with me."

His smile faded. She wasn't ready for him. He stared out the window, not wanting her to see his disappointment.

"Please don't take it the wrong way. I'm excited and scared that you are here, but I don't want to marry a stranger."

He nodded. God gave him the strength to say what she needed to hear. "As you know, my father abused my brother and me. He made me...feel...unworthy. When he joined the army, leaving my mother and his ranch hands take care of the ranch, I had relief. I found out in the six months he was deployed, she had an affair, and my father came back. He was enraged. He started abusing her, calling her a slut..."

###

As Eric shared his secret, Julie's throat ached. Was there something she could do to relieve his suffering? Pray for him? She had and would. Julie had a good upraising. Although her parents had sheltered her, they showed her the love of Christ. Eric had none of that. He had his share of darkness and misery. He and his little brother suffered under the hands of their drunk and abusive father. It had drained her of all that was in her heart. And what about Drew? His mother became pregnant? She needed to share with him, to help him see where she was coming from.

"Since I arrived here, a man has been stalking me. Both Andrew and Beth saw him, but I have not. You are right to say that God is protecting me. Beth told me about Psalms 91, and I meditated on it. Since then, when I start to get into fear, I would get in His presence and the fear would leave."

His mouth dropped open. "Psalms 91?"

"Yes."

"Okay."

Heat radiated in her chest as she continued to share. "Andrew fought for me. He saw what the stalker looked like, and he found out by the license plate on the car that it was rented to...Drew McDermott."

Color drained from his face then his eyes bulged. "I knew it! It was the reason I was so frustrated because I couldn't protect you." The color return to the shade of red, and he covered his mouth. "And you have never seen him?"

"Only sensed his presence. The night my engine died, I felt a chill, but it didn't bother Andrew."

A slow smile built on his face. "Would there be a chance I would see this man—Andrew?"

Her knees weakened. His question took away her concerns. "Are you sure you want to meet him?" She teased. "He might fight for me and win!" She giggled.

A silly grin appeared on his face. "Does he have a gun? We can do an old fashion gun fight. I'm the best gun drawer there is!"

Julie's heart danced. How long had they been on the road? Everything around her faded as she gazed into his eyes. Green like the grass under their feet. Green as emeralds. Too much time had passed, and they needed to get caught up. It was her turn to share.

"I thought I was ready for marriage. We had dated for two years. I thought you would propose, but that phone call happened. I didn't realize until later that the phone call saved me from disappointment. And yes, it was me. I had to. But when I did, it broke me. I wondered how I could do that to you. Two weeks after talking to my pastor, I left town, taking all my flaws with me. Beth said to me that I needed to stop thinking about myself and put myself in others' shoes. Andrew was going to propose, but because I refuse to call my parents, he didn't. Which is a good thing, I think."

"No, I think God kept it from happening." He touched her face, and a pleasurable shiver went up her spine.

"I agree." She smiled.

###

As Eric arrived at Burger World's drive through, all his worries faded into nothingness. She had not seen Drew's face. He could relax. He wanted this moment to last forever. A smile was on her face. A relaxed one.

"Welcome to Burger World! May I take your order?"

"You go ahead," he whispered to Julie.

"I'll have a large chocolate shake and a medium fries."

"Regular or Curly? Seasoned or not?"

"Regular. No season."

Just the way Eric remembered Julie on their second date. He took slow easy breaths as a slight smile appeared on his face...

It was late, but Eric escorted Julie into Julz and Jayz. Amy, a waitress, smiled as she took two menus out of their holder. "Table or booth?"

"Booth," they both said, then they laughed.

Amy knew they didn't smoke, so she led them to a no-smoking area and gave them each a menu. "Can I get you something to drink?"

"Water is fine."

"The same." Julie opened her menu. "Hmm." She had been working here. She would know the menu by heart.
Large chocolate shake and medium fries," she told him.

His limbs tingled. Why was he surprised? "You know the menu, obviously."

"By heart. Their menu's hardly changed, except adding improvement."

He reached to touch her hand. It created a spark, and he smiled.

As he came out of memory lane, happy tears filled his eyes, and his hands tingled as he touched hers. The same spark they had before. His second chance with Julie. "I love you."

Julie had the prettiest of blue eyes, as they glistened like diamonds in the sky. "I love you too." She lowered her voice.

"Can I get your order, sir?"

Huh? He had lost track of time, and he felt heat in his face. "Oh, yes, I'll have the same."

His heart took flight. She loved him. He had won her heart. No—God had loaned her heart to him, for it belonged to God first. He would treasure it and hold it. Who was this Andrew who dared to steal her heart? He reminded her of himself? Really? Did his father have an affair with Andrew's mother? He joked to himself. Not likely that had happened. He still wanted to meet Andrew. He turned the radio and what would you know? A classic song that was just right: "God Blessed the Broken Road" was playing.

"I love how your eyes shine like diamonds in a sea of green," Julie said, not blinking.

His eyes glowed. "Yours shine as the sun in the sky."

She gasped. "Oh, Eric! That is romantic!" She dipped her fry in the ketchup and gave him the first bite, and he savored it.

He drove on.

###

As they listen to country music, her eyes stung with tears. God may have allowed her to leave Montana, but her home and heart were there. Gratitude filled her heart for the friends she had made. Beth, Nate, and of course Andrew...and her new sister! She had forgotten about Vickie! She covered her mouth. "Oh my goodness, I forgot to tell you, but you have to promise not to tell mom and dad!"

He gave her a questionable gaze. "What?"

"Well God showed his goodness in spite of my shortcomings," she giggled. "I have a sister!"

His eyes shot big with surprise. Or was it disbelief? "You have a... sister?"

"I know. I couldn't believe it! You have to meet her! She was how I got my job! She works as the manager of Books and Gifts. If the previous employer hadn't have resigned, I would not have a job."

"God is amazing!" He smiled. "So how was it that it came up or you found out?"

"My last name rang a bell with her. She asked me if my parents were Earl and Eleanor, which I said yes. I was shocked too. They had given her up for adoption after she was born."

"I know your folks aren't well off, but they were content."

"They taught me contentment too. I didn't realize deep down inside I harbored jealousy and envy until I saw what my new friends had." A tear fell, but he wiped it.

"You have so much more than you know. The apostle wrote that he knew the secret of contentment. I love his writings."

Warmth surged through her limbs. In her heart, Julie worshipped God. Was this how Philemon felt when he receive back Onesimus? Although she ran away, it was God who had brought Eric back to her. A new man. A new creation. A man after her own heart. How could she give thanks to God who had worked this out for her?

"Hope deferred makes the heart sick, but longing fulfilled is a tree life." She let that verse sink it.

"Amen!" he smiled. "Amen!"

Chapter 19

As they watched a romantic movie, Julie leaned into Eric's arms. Her chest fluttered. Eric would stay at Motel 8 for a week, then he had to return to Montana. Julie would return too, but not with him. She needed to give Vickie a two weeks' notice before she resigned. Since she gave her previous employers a chance to find a replacement, they could hire her again. She could move out of her parents' house and find her own place.

"I need to call my parents."

"That would be a good idea." He checked the time on his watch. "It's almost eleven over there."

"Is it that late already?"

Eric had a silly grin on his face. "I know! Where did time fly, right?" He chuckled.

"Right!" She snuggled in his arms. "I miss this."

"Do you realize something?"

"What's that?"

"We are watching a movie in your house. No Craig. He's in jail, and I am not going to bail him out." He gazed at Julie. "And you won't bail out on me either, right?"

As he removed a small red box, her heart pounded. She prayed that no phone call would ruin this moment. She hadn't sensed any danger since his arrival, but it could happen. *Please God! Keep Drew away.* If he did come, she had no doubts that Eric could defeat him. Andrew was from the city. He would be no match for Drew because deep inside her heart, she knew God could give Eric the power to defeat him. Eric would do it for God. To defeat Drew for her.

"Julie Henshaw, if you want a long engagement, we could have one. Two years we both weren't ready, but we are now. At least I hope so. Will you do me the honor of becoming a wife and making my last name yours?"

Tears streamed down her face, and her muscles trembled. God had kept Andrew from proposing so he could reunite her with Eric. All this time, God had other plans for her. Locking him away for life so she could date someone was not the plan. Beth's words came rushing to her: *God allowed you to come so he can work on both of your hearts.* "Yes. We can make it long." As she kissed his sweet lips of love, he drew her in with his kiss.

"When will Beth be back?" he asked in between kisses.

"Who cares?"

He chuckled. "Mmm hmm."

###

His heart leapt with joy. The woman of his dreams said yes. No more life of loneliness. He would have a partner by his side. She could help him on the ranch and be the mother of his children. How would she feel about going home for good? Or would she rather live here? *.I have to make sure Drew doesn't get the ranch.* He brushed her long hair aside.

"How do you feel about ranching in California?"

She sat up, giving him a disbelieving look. "You would have to leave Randy and John behind. They're your friends."

"Yes, but you made California home."

She touched his lips, which gave him pleasure. "Temporary home. My home will be with you. We could live in South Dakota for all we care."

He held her face in his hands. "You don't know how happy I am, but being with you surpasses it all. Please say it again. I might be dreaming."

She pinched him.

"Hey!"

"I guess you're not dreaming," She giggled.

"Oh yeah?"

When she saw the teasing look in his eyes, she got up and started to run, but he overtook her and locked her in his arms. "I hope this feeling never goes away."

"What feeling is that?" he asked.

"Love, euphoria. I have never felt this good in all my life." She gazed into his eyes,

He turned around and held her. Her lips begging him to kiss her. She hoped he would, that he didn't want to let her go.

###

"Hello?" Julie's voice woke him. "Who is this...Whoever this is better stop it—"

Eric took the phone from her hand, feeling protective. "Whoever this is better hang up now!"

"You ain't seen the last of me, Young!" *Click*.

Eric counted to ten before he reacted. Drew had no business calling. *God, you said in your word that vengeance is mine. You also said do not sin when you are angry, but I need help now!* Eric wanted to bash Drew's brain in.

Julie's eyes showed shock. "Who was it? Drew?"

He calmed his heart. "Yes, but you don't need to worry about him." He touched her face, as her eyes showed concern, but not fear. "God and I are here."

Love was in her eyes. "I'm safe because of both of you."

###

When they arrived at Books and Gifts, surprise tingled in his neck. *She works here?* A small building sandwiched between two other small stores. Bozeman had a few business like that too. Neck to neck as he would call it.

Inside, soft music poured from the backroom while display racks held audiocassettes, DVDs, and vintage video cassettes. No one played videocassettes anymore. He browsed through them.

"Vickie, this is my man from Montana."

She caught his attention, and he smiled at the woman with light brown hair pulled back in a braid. She didn't have blue eyes like Julie, but her lips were the same as the bone structure on Julie's face. "Hi, I'm Eric." He shook her warm hand. She has a good heart.

Her eyes danced with delight. "Nice to meet you."

"I have a favor to ask," Julie hedged.

"What's that?" Vickie responded.

"I would like a vacation time."

His heart dashed to pieces. She wasn't going to ask for two weeks' notice? She had led him to believe she wanted to go home. His smile faded.

Vickie gasped at seeing Julie's ring. "He proposed?"

Julie beamed. "Yes. Andrew was for a season. I'm glad God sent him my way." She smiled back at Eric then at Vickie. "But Eric is for me. I agreed to a long engagement, but I need to see my family. May I have next week off?"

"Yes. Beth will be back, and April is here." Julie had told him that she hired April last month and that she felt led to have one more employee.

"She's the new assistant!" Julie responded then gave Eric a hug. "He's staying a week, I thought we could return together. It would do my family good to see us together."

"You got it girl!"

His heart soared. She wanted to come back with him, even for a week. He could have her to himself. She could help him on the ranch. He could have her in his house and take her for a ride on Prince. Someday she would have a horse of her own. A white horse, because in his eyes, she was like the lily of the valley and the fresh snow that fell on the ground. White, the color of purity. And on their wedding day, when she walked down the aisle, she would grace them all with her pure heart and pure love for him. She would be his eternally. "I love you."

She held him, gazing at him. "I'm yours." Her smile reached her eyes.

He kissed her lips. "I'll let you work. I think I will explore your town and around. Maybe find a ranch to help out on."

"Beth has a friend that lives on a farm. Her name is Holly."

"She does, does she?" He kissed her again. "Ciao for now." He skipped out of the store.

###

"Wow!" Vickie mouth dropped open. "He's quite a cowboy."

Julie thrusted her chest out as she beamed. "Yes, indeed he is."

Vickie burst out into laughter, and soon April came out and joined in. "April, Eric came all the way from my home state and Julie's home state to propose to Julie." She gave a joyful laugh.

All three bumped each other in merriment.

###

A black pickup truck passed Beth as she arrived at Books and Gifts. Her breath stalled. Was that Eric? Was he in town?" She ran inside, and the three women were dancing and laughing. Why weren't they working? "Hello." She raised her eyebrows.

Julie ran to her. "Oh Beth! Oh Beth! Look!" She showed her ring to Beth.

"Congratulations. When's the big day?" Beth went to sign in, struggling to keep envy at bay. She didn't want to disappoint Julie.

"Beth, what's going on? You seem sad."

"Nate broke up with me."

Julie gasped. "I'm sorry. Did he say why?"

"It's what I suspected. He is noncommittal, and I put the pressure on him. I told him I wanted to marry."

"Oh, Beth! I'm so sorry." She gave Beth a hug.

Trying to put it behind her, she said, "So the black truck that left is his?"

Julie beamed. "You saw his truck? Yes! We went on our first date last night—but now you are my concern. How can I help you feel better?"

Vickie came in. "We have customers waiting."

"I'll be out there," Julie said. "I would like you and Vickie be my bridesmaids."

Beth's heart warmed. "I would be honored." She walked around Julie.

###

Beth's disappointment weighed on Julie's heart. Was there something she could do to help her friend? How ironic that she was about to break up with Andrew, and Nate did it to Beth. Maybe the twins weren't for them. *It would be a bad idea to invite her to have lunch with us.* Would Eric understand? *Lord prepare his heart.*

Throughout the morning, Beth remained quiet, still sad about the breakup. She tried to put on a brave smile for the customers, but Julie saw her heart.

An hour before lunchtime, Julie caught her breath as she picked up whistling outside. Drew had called earlier, and she suspected the whistling came from him.

"Drew?" Beth whispered.

Julie nodded as she kept her eye on the door. If Eric couldn't come to her rescue God would. She reached for her phone and checked the time and her messages. Julie sent Eric a message. "He's here."

"On my way!" He texted back.

Julie stood firm as she manned her station. "We should call the police. They are still looking for him." Julie got on her cell phone and held out her hand as Beth opened her mouth.

"Marysville Police Department. Captain Holland speaking. May I help you?"

"Drew McDermott is at Books and Gifts. Can you get him?"

"We're on our way!"

Their answer gave Julie the relief she needed. "He's on his way."

"Can you keep him busy until they come?"

"I'm protected, Beth."

"Did you tell Eric about him?" Beth raised her eyebrows.

"Yes. He said Drew was his half-brother."

Beth gasped. "No. Get out of here!" she whispered.

Vickie had put up the "Out to Lunch" sign as on cue. "Let's go, ladies. Let's have lunch on me."

Beth perked up. "Yes! That sounds good."

"Eric and the police are on their way."

"That man is out there!" Beth said, shocked.

"God is with me." Julie smiled.

"God bless you." Vickie led the others out the back.

A few minutes later, the doorknob jiggled, and she saw his face. She stood tall and strong, trying to fight off the fear that wanted to rise in her. "The Lord is my shepherd, I shall not want..."

The sound of sirens grew loud and wheels screeched.

"He leads me beside still waters..."

"YOU'RE UNDER ARREST! PUT YOUR HANDS UP WHERE WE CAN SEE THEM!"

Julie's knees weakened. Her light had come. They arrested Drew.

"Julie, open up! It's me, Eric!"

And Eric was here. She collapsed to the floor; happy tears streaking her face. "Thank you, Jesus!"

###

As the police handcuffed him, Drew's heart pounded in his ears. He swore Eric would pay for this and so would Julie. One day he would get what was coming to him, and he would regret it for the rest of his life.

The police read him his rights, but he could care less. He trusted no one, not even Lydia. She had ratted on him, but Julie had Drew arrested. *She will pay!* They forced him into the car, lowering his head. His neck corded.

###

Julie sent a text to Andrew. "Drew is arrested."

He texted back. " 😮"

She gave him a smiley.

Eric knocked at the door, and she rushed to let him in. "I saw him getting in the car." A smile danced on his lips, and they puckered for a kiss.

Julie's heart danced. Her lips found a way to his She wrapped her arms around him. "Mmm hmm."

"But for how long?" he asked between kisses.

Julie pulled away. "Good question. He hadn't done anything worse than stalking me."

He held her close, smelling her scent, and she giggled. "You smell good."

She closed her eyes. He smelled of love. "Thank you. Are you hungry?"

"Famished." He brushed back her hair as he brushed his lips against hers. "Especially for love. I missed you so much. Want to go to Denny's?"

"How about a drive thru? We can go in your truck."

"I thought you would never ask."

She ran to the back to get her purse then followed Eric out as she locked the front door. "You missed Beth. She came back disappointed. I felt heartbroken."

He helped her climbed in his truck. "Why? What happened?"

"Nate, her boyfriend, broke up with her. They had dated off and on."

"I'm sorry to hear." He climbed in on his side.

As Eric drove, her throat ached. She left Montana, but he gave her a second chance. Beth had done nothing to have her heart broken. Why did she continue to date Nate if he was only interested in having girlfriends? Wasn't there someone special for her? Julie closed her eyes as her lips parted. "Jesus, Beth needs you. She is hurting. Is there someone out there for her?" Beth was appealing to the eye. She stood tall and slender, an overall pleasant expression on her face. The light of Christ shone brightly in her eyes. Was this why Beth had resented her good fortune? But Julie didn't keep Andrew long, did she? Both men lost their women.

Julie barked a laugh. "Nate doesn't deserve Beth."

"I didn't deserve you. Someday, Nate will realize what he lost."

"That's true, isn't it? If he would just settle down."

"Give them time." His eyes softened and glowed as he patted her leg.

Chapter 20

As Julie packed for her vacation, her arm itched. She put on some lotion, but it didn't soothed the itch. *Did they release Drew?* Vandalism was not as serious of a crime as murder. What if they released him the next day? Did he pay bail? Her stomach hurt.

The screeching of wheels hurt her ears. The slamming of a car door caught her attention. Outside, Eric climbed out of his car and fury was on his face. It did not look good.

Julie opened the door as he stormed up the walk. "What's wrong?"

"They released him on bail." His nostrils flared.

"No!"

He held her in his arms. "I'm glad you are leaving with me."

"Remember, God is my protection."

He nodded. "Hopefully he won't follow us. I also found this on my truck." He handed her a note.

"Because she had me arrested, your ranch will suffer. I have allies." Julie glanced at Eric. "Allies?"

"It could just be a threat."

###

Julie's heart pounded like a judge's gavel. Who did Drew think he was? Who gave him power to make threats against them? "Please tell me why again?" She raised her voice.

"He has been this way since he was old enough to know right from wrong. Maybe it's because I'm my father's son."

"But why does he want the ranch?" Her eyes bulged.

"Inheritance."

It all made sense to her. Eric had inherited the ranch because he was the oldest. It would be giving away his birthright. Eric had to keep the ranch or lose his birthright. She needed to stand by her man. "Well, you know what? There are more on our side than there are on his!" She placed her hands on her hips.

A smile danced on his lips. "I love your fire. I think red hair suits you fine." She felt a shiver of pleasure as he brushed her hair back. "Are you ready, my fearless princess?"

"Almost ready."

He let her go so she could pack. "I appreciate you letting me drive us."

"I'll just have to take a plane back." She put in the last of her toiletries and zipped in her suitcase. "Beth wanted to know if I would be leaving for good. I told her in the future."

"Have you finished paying off the mortgage of your house?"

"No, and that is why I want to wait. I don't want to leave her with the mortgage." She said as he took out his checkbook. "What are you doing?"

"I want to help, but it won't be much."

"You don't have to."

"I want to." After he filled a check out, he pulled her to himself and gazed into her eyes. "You owe me nothing. I'm doing it because I love you." He kissed her hand, causing the hair on her hand to bristle.

She smiled. "I love you too. So are we going to have faith the ranch will be okay?"

His eyes danced with merriment. "If he burns it, he burns it. My men may be out of a job, but I'm not going to let a threat come between us."

Julie smiled as she followed Eric to his truck.

###

As Eric drove off with Julie in the front seat, Drew's ears roared. Drew's dark heart planned its course. Eric would not heed the note, as he had driven away from Julie's home. If a ranch on fire wouldn't divert Eric's course, then perhaps, getting to him through Julie would quench Drew's desire to ruin Eric. What would be dear to Julie? Her friends?

Beth had seen his eyes, had she? Perhaps he could use Beth for his advantage. She had seemed a little disappointed as he entered her workplace. A breakup? Why not exact revenge by using Beth against Julie?

"I've seen that look in your eyes before," Lydia laughed

"You know me, Darling. I never give up." He kissed her lips, but spat after that. She disgusted him. A whore that he was using. "Let's follow the lovebirds, shall we?"

"Yes."

He zoomed away.

###

That night, Beth tried to slow her breathing as she unlocked the door. A cat running across her path caused her to jump. "Stupid cat!" She let herself in and closed the door and flicked on the lights. "Julie, are you here?" She placated.

She took out her gun as she made her way to her bedroom. Keeping her eyes on her surrounding, her breath caught. A rectangular, flat object lay on the table. A check? Upon closer inspection, she lifted her eyebrows. Eric had written her a check for one thousand dollars! It lay next to a note from Julie.

Beth,

Be on guard. They arrested Drew, but he is out on bail. Eric left you a gift to help pay the mortgage. Please accept and see you next week.

Love you, Julie.

A shiver of delight tingled on her skin. Julie and Eric had thought of her. All week, she didn't have the energy or willpower to go to work, and she struggled with church. Did Julie pray for her? Julie never judged her when Beth resented her good fortune. She showed unconditional love. She wished she had met Eric, but Julie had spent every day with him and mostly when she was away. She would have to meet him another time.

They shared many days fellowshipping with each other. God had answered her prayers by giving her a like-minded roommate. She would miss Julie after she moved. Someday she would pay them a visit.

"God, thank you for Julie. Thank you for sending her into my life. Please guard and protect her." She took a deep breath

The check took her mind off the uneasy feeling she'd had, and she would not let fear in again. It was time for Julie True.

Chapter 21

As Eric drove down I-80, Julie's insides felt like they were vibrating. Manure and the agricultural area smell of home. He had called her parents and said he was coming and he had a surprise for them. Were they gasping and thinking of her? They hadn't seen her for over one year. Had it been that long?

And she couldn't wait to see them. Tears poured like rain on a dry land. She had missed her parents. As overprotective as they were, they loved her and doted on her. She wanted to hug them and tell them how much she loved them.

Eric held her close, smiling at her. "I didn't say what the surprise was, but I think they suspected you."

Julie wiped her eyes. "I couldn't even call them. They blamed me for what happened. I'm glad you told them not to fault me."

"Tell me something, sweetheart. Have I ever laid a hand on you?" He wiped a stray tear.

"No and I don't blame you either. When I heard your voicemail, a floodgate of tears opened up."

"Aww. I love you, sweetie." He kissed her face.

"Do you think we will revive them?"

"Yes I believe so. They have always been for us."

###

Her parents waited outside as they arrived at her house. Eleanor covered her mouth and a wide smile appeared on her father's face. Julie's chest drummed as she embraced her mom. No longer did she feel the shame of what she had done or have regrets of breaking her parents' hearts. They welcomed her with open arms and tears of joy.

"Julie, baby, we missed you!" Her father embraced her.

"Look at you! You dyed your hair!" Her mother gasped.

Julie pulled herself away as her mother and father beamed. "Eric said it's perfect for me."

Her mother looked fondly at Eric. "Thank you."

"That's *part* of the surprise. Look at her finger." Eric hinted.

Julie showed them her ring.

They had no words, only tears. Finally, her forty-eight-year-old mother and fifty-two-year-old father leapt and danced as they shouted, "Hallelujah!"

Joy and gladness filled Julie's heart, and Eric beamed as he watched the display. "I think we revived them," Julie said.

###

A melody played on Eric's heart. The object of his desire gazed into his eyes. Her eyes shone as the sun in the sky. Her pearly whites as the gates of eternal bliss, eternal happiness. Julie was his and would always be his. Whoever this Andrew was, he had lost her fair and square. He really had no chance since God was on their side. "I still haven't met Andrew."

"I called him on the way here. He was a little disappointed, but he will get over it." Her mouth curved into a smile. "Andrew is a good guy. He has his faults, but his good qualities make up for them just as yours do."

His heart warmed. "Aww. I love you." He drew her in for a kiss.

###

The chicken cooking in the oven and the sweet smell of cinnamon baked into an apple pie filled the air. Julie breathed in the scent of the home-cooked meal. There was nothing like having a big meal with family, especially with Eric by her side.

"Your momma and I are worn out all from all that dancing. No wonder I don't dance anymore!" Her father roared with laughter and everyone joined in

"Thinking of dancing, I got to do a little slow dancing in California."

"You must tell us about California." Her mother joined them on the couch. "Are you going back?"

"She is on vacation, but she'll move back." Eric caressed her face, which gave her a jolt.

"Yes. I wanted you to see us like this. I left California because I couldn't face you and Eric. But I realized that God allowed it to happen. He changed both our hearts." She exchange glances with Eric then smiled to her parents. "After we are married, I might see if I can get a part-time job for later in the day. I want to be his helpmate."

"And I look forward to that." He gave her a squeeze.

"Marysville is not as rural as Bozeman, but I would visit there and my soul sister."

"Soul sister?"

"We have a kindred spirit."

After they had a meal together, Eric yawned. "I need to get to the ranch. It's late." He kissed Julie's lip. "See me off?"

"Yes." She smiled. She got up and walked him to the door.

Eric gazed at her. "I don't want to impose. If you ever want to come and see me, call me. I'm sure Randy or John would be glad to pick you up."

"I will do that. Don't be a stranger."

"Same with you." He pulled her in for a kiss, and they lingered until he broke free, as his eyes wanted to close. "Good night, darling."

"Good night."

That night, the stars shone bright as hope and love filled her heart. Tomorrow would be a new day for Julie Henshaw.

Epilogue

Butterflies danced as Julie wiped her sweaty palms on her white, satiny wedding dress with lacy hems and necklines and a veil to cover her face. In just a few minutes, she would be walking down the aisle, soon to become Julie Young. She loved the sound of that.

Beth handed her a pearl bracelet. "Something new. I saw it at the boutique. Has your name on it."

Julie's breath stalled as each of the five pearls had spelled out her name. "Wow! Thank you." She put it on.

"Something old." Her mother gave her a brooch with small, little diamonds on it. "Used to be your grandmother's. I wore it on my wedding day."

Julie pinned it on her dress.

"Something borrowed." Jordan gave her a necklace with small rhinestones on it.

"It's gorgeous."

"And something blue." Charity gave her a garter to put around her leg.

"Ladies, five minutes!" Earl called.

"I can't believe this day is happening!" Tears streamed down Julie's face. "I have waited for this day for over two years! God you are so good!"

"Amen!" they all said.

###

As the music played, Eric swallowed a shout of glee. He wanted to maintain his composure. Had he ever thought this day would happen? Two years ago his world fell apart when Julie left him, and his hopes were dashed when the police found the body, but God had worked it out. Randy had hired an attorney for him who had gotten him a deal to turn in Craig Muldare for a shorter sentence. He had to because his love for Julie was stronger than his loyalty to his friend. He had wanted her in his life because she was his world. He had it wrong. God was his world. Jesus was his life, and Eric and Julie would partner with God.

Julie took his breath away as she strolled down the aisle. Her father at her right hand, beaming and looking more proud than he ever had. She graced the walkway with her purity and her beauty.

The double doors opened, and Vickie stepped in and walked quietly to the bride's side but not toward the front. She looked as though she wanted to remain inconspicuous. Julie had told him that she would be there late. At least she made it. She smiled when he had smiled to her.

The scent of vanilla filled his nostrils as Julie joined him at his side.

###

The prison guard came to his cell, and Drew's heart pounded. Would he have a visitor? Or was this an early release?

"You have a visitor." He unlocked Drew's cell and handcuffed him.

"A visitor? Who?"

"Matthew Young."

His stomach fluttered. After six months, his other half-brother had come to visit him. Would he have good news about the ranch? Matthew worked for Eric and was his eyes while he was a way. The prison guard placed him on the other side of the divider, but Matthew wasn't there. He turned to the guard. "Where is he?"

"They're bringing him now."

The door opened, and a guard led a shorter man with short, dark brown hair to a seat opposite him.

"Hey there!" Matthew sat down.

He leaned forward. "You have news?"

Mathew's eyes shone with confidence. "Not the kind of news you want. The ranch is still there. Julie is still in California." He raised his eyebrows. "How did you get here?"

Julie had put him here, and his heart roared in his ears. She sealed her fate the day she called the police. All he wanted to do was to stop by and say hi. He guessed that Beth gal had put her up to it. Beth may have seen his eyes, but she had not seen Brad. He had dark plans for her and Julie. "Julie put me here." He cussed.

"Why? You haven't done anything to her, have you?" Surprise was in his eyes.

Drew's cold heart warmed. Matthew was on his side and not on his brother's. He would do what he could to ruin Eric for how he had allowed his mother's husband to abuse Matthew. "You're darn right. I have six months left then I'm back in Montana." He said no more. Walls have ears. Someone on the other side could thwart his plans if they knew. He was thirsty for power and control. He hungered for revenge, and he would have it.

"Be my eyes until I am free. I'm stuck here for six months more."

Matthew smiled as he nodded. "I'm here for you, bro."

Julie ain't seen the last of him yet.

Dear Readers,

I hope you've enjoyed The Past Hunter: Two Men: Her Past and Present. It took me a long time to rewrite it, but with the seventh anniversary coming up, God gave me the peace to write a second edition. If you read the first and wrote a review, I hope you will leave one for the second edition. My love for ranchers and Montana inspired me to write this book. I hope you fall in love with my characters. If you read the original and didn't leave a review, I hope you will for this one. I hope this story touches your heart. Please leave a review for me at Amazon and Goodreads (If you have marked it as currently reading) Thank you.

Because I had to rewrite book one, **Baby Blues** won't be re-released until next year. I had introduced the real villain in book one so it changes book 2. A Man For Beth is available at Amazon. Following after The Past Hunter, I will re-release **A Second Chance at Love** with a new cover and much improve storyline. Do you like Ted Dekker and Frank Parretti, then you will enjoy Purify My Heart

Visit Me:
Madison Books on Facebook

I welcome emails!
ruthie@ruthiemadison.com No hate mails, please!

Would you like to join my street team? Go to Facebook.com and enter Author Ruthie Madison Street Team in search bar.

Acknowledgment

Every good and perfect gift comes from the Father of heavenly lights, the almighty God. He first endowed my late grandmother Ruth McLeod and got passed down to me. Yet all inspiration comes from God alone. I would also like to acknowledge Elizabeth Derby for her support and encouragement. Where would I be without her? When I felt like giving up, she would encourage me not to and give me advice when I needed it. I would also like to thank my fans and readers. I would not be writing if it wasn't for the reviews you leave and the support you have given me. Thank you!

Made in the USA
Monee, IL
18 October 2026

66035035R00080